NEW YORK REVIEW BOOKS
CLASSICS

THE WEDDING OF ZEIN

TAYEB SALIH (1929–2009) was born in northern Sudan and educated at the University of Khartoum. After a brief period working as a teacher, he moved to London to work with the BBC Arabic Service. Salih later worked as director general of information in Qatar in the Arabian Gulf, and then with UNESCO in Paris and the Arab Gulf States. Along with *The Wedding of Zein*, his books in English include *Season of Migration to the North* (also published as an NYRB Classic) and *Bandarshah*.

DENYS JOHNSON-DAVIES has translated more than thirty-five books by modern Arab authors, including Naguib Mahfouz and Mahmoud Darwish. He has also produced more than fifty books for children, mostly taken from traditional Arabic sources. He was recently awarded the Sheikh Zayed Prize for his services to Arabic literature. He lives in Cairo.

HISHAM MATAR was born in 1970 in New York City to Libyan parents and spent his childhood in Tripoli and Cairo. His first novel, *In the Country of Men* (2006), was short-listed for the Man Booker Prize. He lives in London.

THE WEDDING OF ZEIN

And Other Stories

TAYEB SALIH

Translated from the Arabic by

DENYS JOHNSON-DAVIES

Introduction by

HISHAM MATAR

Illustrated by

IBRAHIM SALAHI

NEW YORK REVIEW BOOKS

New York

THIS IS A NEW YORK REVIEW BOOK
PUBLISHED BY THE NEW YORK REVIEW OF BOOKS
435 Hudson Street, New York, NY 10014
www.nyrb.com

This collection was first published in Beirut, Lebanon, as '*Urs al-Zayn: Sab'
qiṣaṣ,* 1962. First published in this translation in the Heinemann African
Writers Series, 1969.

"The Doum Tree of Wad Hamid" first appeared in this translation in
Encounter, November 1962. "A Handful of Dates" first appeared in this translation in *Encounter*, January 1966.

Library of Congress Cataloging-in-Publication Data
Salih, al-Tayyib.
['Urs al-Zayn: sab' qiṣaṣ. English]
The wedding of Zein / by Tayeb Salih ; translated by Denys Johnson-Davies.
   p. cm.
ISBN 978-1-59017-342-8 (alk. paper)
I. Johnson-Davies, Denys. II. Title.
PJ7862.A564M313 2010
892.7'36—dc22

                    2009036057

ISBN 978-1-59017-342-8

Printed in the United States of America on acid-free paper.
10 9 8 7 6 5

Contents

Introduction

In the opening chapters of the nineteenth century the Ottoman sultan's viceroy in Egypt, Muhammad Ali Pasha, ordered his troops south. They rode behind the pasha's son into Nubia and farther down into the heartland of the Sudan, where they seized the province of Kordofan. They then turned east into the state of Sennar. Such was the painful birth of modern Sudan.

Paradoxically, the invaders' actions had the effect of uniting the native farmers, merchants, and tribesmen in resistance to them, thus planting the seed of the Mahdist Revolution that, sixty years later, in 1881, erupted in that same central Kordofan province. The Mahdists snatched the country out of the mighty claws of the British Empire, which by then controlled Egypt and with it the Sudan. That a collection of untrained people armed with swords, sticks, and spears had defeated the large modern army deployed by Britain shocked the Western world. It heralded the turning of the colonial tide and inspired subsequent indigenous armed liberation movements. In 1883 the Sudan had become the first and, as it turned out, the only African country to have expelled a colonial power by force of arms. But after a brief interlude, the troops of a humiliated Britain, based at Wadi Halfa, a town not far from the village where Tayeb Salih was born, struck back, and in 1899 colonial rule was reinstated in the form of the Anglo-Egyptian Condominium.

The glories and disasters of the Mahdist State and the various forms of foreign rule the country endured helped cement national identity and stimulated Sudanese nationalism. On New Year's Day 1956 the largest country in Africa gained its independence, a country that is Arab in the flat plains of the north and African in the verdant south.

Arab and African, Muslim, animist and Christian currents have run through the Sudan for more than a thousand years. Their incomplete fusion explains the existential isolation that the Sudanese endure in relation to the Arab world: in almost every interview he ever gave, Salih found need to assert his Arabness. The geography of the Sudan adds to the complexity of the nation. It shares a border with no less than nine countries: Eritrea and Ethiopia to the East; Kenya, Uganda, and the Democratic Republic of the Congo to the south; the Central African Republic, Chad, and Libya to the West; and to the north the country's closest cultural neighbor, Egypt, where, after the Blue and White Niles merge in the Sudanese capital, Khartoum, the one river continues.

———

In the winter of 1953, three years before the Sudan gained its independence, Tayeb Salih came to London. Behind him was a "story of spectacular success at school" in his provincial northern farming village by the Nile, then university in Khartoum, where he later worked as a schoolteacher. A quiet and naturally self-deprecating manner did not foretell the luminous talent he sheltered. The only thing that might have suggested his gifts was a vague yet persistent aloofness, as if he had decided long ago to give very little away, to live primarily within solitude's faithful chamber.

I wonder how that first journey to the English capital was for the twenty-four-year-old. I suspect that like the enigmatic Mustafa Sa'eed in Salih's masterful novel *Season of Migration to the North*, the young author had also traveled up from Khartoum to Egypt and then boarded a ship for Dover. He may have found the waterscape oddly familiar—just as Mustafa Sa'eed does. To his ears the new country must have sounded crisp, dustless. And as the pitched roofs of the first houses appeared they would have reminded him of the bony backs of the Nile buffalo. England would have seemed a precise universe in which every structure, field, and tree had been allocated a specific place. Water here did not run in crooked streams but was trapped to flow politely within man-made banks. Trains sliced the landscape and when they stopped, they stopped for a measured interval, just long enough to allow passengers to hurry off and on. "No fuss," as Sa'eed puts it.

No fuss is one of the advantages of being away from home. If writing is the discovery of the self, it is also its reinvention. A process aided by exile's anonymity. In Salih's case the life of an exile was to stretch until February 2009, when he died in the London home he shared with his English wife and their three daughters. Apart from a few years spent in Doha as director general of the Qatari Ministry of Information and ten years in Paris working for UNESCO, Salih spent the majority of the fifty-six years that followed his departure from the Sudan in London, from where he contributed weekly reviews, literary journalism, and political commentary to *Al-Majalla* magazine. All these "proper" jobs caused some Arab artists and intellectuals to accuse him of not being committed to his art. On the day of his death that ended. Obituaries flowed in from every corner, confirming his place in the canon. The business of how the writer got his living was no longer there to distract his readers from the greatness of his work.

———

The novella "The Wedding of Zein," published here along with two short stories, "The Doum Tree of Wad Hamid" and "A Handful of Dates," first appeared in 1962, nine years into the author's new life in London. I cannot find fault with the exquisite English translation. The Canadian Denys Johnson-Davies lived in the Sudan as a child, which gives him an insider's ear for the colloquial turns of phrase that are sometimes employed by Salih in dialogue.

Unlike Salih's better-known work, *Season of Migration to the North*, which was published four years later in 1966 and tells the story of an Arab African negotiating existence in the West, these three narratives show characters in their native setting. Here local life is yet to be punctured by the new postindependence central government and yet to be challenged by Westernized compatriots returning from abroad. Khartoum is as far away as London. Instead, these perfectly shaped vernacular narratives take place within the confines of a Sudanese village that is not dissimilar from Salih's birthplace. Though the villagers know nothing of the world outside the village, and though that world has not yet sought to place its mark on village life, they know it is there, and they know that it has designs upon them. This subtle yet persistent tension between village life and the outer world that Salih evokes gives his stories, and "The Wedding of Zein" in particular, an anxious, nocturnal quality. It is as if every character is secretly nursing the conviction that their way of life is under threat. For example, when "the gang," those influential men of the village, gathers late at night, an uncanny image is created:

> ...light from the lamp touched them with the tip of its tongue. Sometimes, when they were plunged in laughter, the light and shadow danced above their heads as though they were immersed in a sea in which they floated and dipped.

We wonder what it signifies. Modernity, perhaps, with its foreign illuminations? Or something else? But before our questions can be resolved, Salih moves on: "where does the lamplight end? how does the darkness begin?"

Salih believed symbolism in fiction ought to be like "something buried, reflecting dark rays that are at times contradictory." His ability to do this, to create a work that is both realist and magical, allegorical and endlessly elusive, is one of his achievements and why perhaps Salih has had more than his fair share of critics bent on subjecting his work to reductive readings. Though his work has inspired some nuanced and illuminating studies, it has also, perhaps more than the work of any other Arab novelist, suffered at the hands of readers less interested in the author's art than in finding support for their opinions.

Although these stories are a happy reflection on what the author once described as "a world [that] was fast disappearing," they are also a lament. They mark the point just before the author surrendered altogether to loss, before he dropped the flint and took only to pondering "how does the darkness begin." These early stories, with their undertones of satire and hints of Beckettian absurdity, are in no sense sentimental or satisfied. "The Wedding of Zein" is narrated with a nearly cruel detachment. But even that is a kind of trick, Salih's way of leaving us to our own conclusions. This is an author who always knows how and when to get out of the way. Salih's nostalgia is most powerful when he writes about nature, which inspires passages of raw pastoral beauty. Guided in the dark by distant sounds of merriment, Zein comes to the river:

> The Nile's breast, like that of a man in anger, swells up, and the water flows over its banks.

And,

> The land is motionless and moist, yet you feel that its belly encases a great secret, as though it were a woman of boundless passion preparing to meet her mate.

In "The Wedding of Zein," nature is both matter-of-fact and full of amoral determination. The earth throbs with sexual desire and mystery. It exists primarily for itself, continuously working toward its own ends. It is by no means a pretty backdrop but a psychological force. And if we see Zein, what with his wild abandon and wily ability to elude many of society's rules, as an expression of nature's will, then "The Wedding of Zein" can be read as a chronicle of nature's quiet victory: how the village fool triumphs, without seeming to try, in winning the heart of "the most beautiful of them all," the lovely, independent-minded, intelligent Ni'ma, the cousin who, in her Koranic studies, pictured mercy as a woman, and wished she had been named Mercy instead. In marrying Zein she is sacrificing herself to nature, as perhaps everything of worth in the young Sudan must lie at the mercy of the unknowable future.

Right from the start of "The Wedding of Zein" we know we are dealing with an unusual hero, one who came out of his mother's womb and immediately "burst out laughing." He is deformed, even grotesque, has only two teeth, one on top, the other on the bottom, but when people mock him he giggles. This even though he has a Herculean strength. He loves parties, detects a distant wedding the way an animal sniffs out a prey. He threatens divorce even though he is not married. He is struck on the head with an ax, but when the wound heals it improves his looks.

Since independence, Arab societies have been plagued by the intoxicating hope that a great national savior will come and fix everything. Salih touches on this futile and absurd dream when Zein's kindness and heroism cause the villagers to wonder if he "was the legendary Leader, the Prophet... sent down by God." But when Zein returns to his tomfoolery this fantasy is "destroyed and replaced" by one "to which people were accustomed and which they preferred."

Zein's dervish status makes him as inoffensive as a child, allowing him to pinch the ladies' behinds without incurring too much reproach, while elevating him to the role of a spiritual weathervane. However, Zein's most important function in the eyes of the villagers is to serve "as a trumpet by which attention was drawn to their daughters." His love blesses. No sooner does he yell his comical "O people, she has slain me" than his tormenting beloved turns into the most eligible bride in the village.

The shamelessness of Zein's loves, and the way his fiery passions fade the minute his beloved is married off, hint at a Sufi theme: that all earthly longing is but a metaphor for the boundless love of the divine. Salih took an interest in Sufi mysticism. Sufism places great emphasis on the sacredness of the present moment, in which, it is believed, the world is remade entire. We never witness Zein regretting the past or worrying about the future. Salih links Sufi logic with a pastoral vision of nature that is no less preoccupied with the present. The only time Zein is nudged out of the present is when his own love is at last satisfied. He leaves his wedding party to go weep by the grave of his friend, the holy mystic Haneen, who had "perceived in [Zein] a glimmering of spiritual light." After he has reminded himself of his true longing, he returns to dance with complete abandon.

For many Arab writers of the mid-twentieth century Sufism, with its familiar philosophical terrain, served as a helpful way to engage the new secular modernism without severing ties to premodern homelands and traditions.

The narrative in "The Wedding of Zein" circles around itself: an incident is hinted at and later the picture is filled in; then we return to the incident again, but now seeing it under a different light or from a another perspective. These retellings make the fictional world at once more familiar and yet less solid and predictable. Thanks to this technique, and thanks to his distilled prose, Salih's work establishes a peculiar tension between the limited nature of human experience and its infinite depth.

Salih's style, unlike that of so many Arab novelists of his generation, is neither verbose nor lush. All his sentences are cut short with a thin wire of grief. Perhaps every writer who wants to write unsentimentally, to write deeply, about his country needs what Mustafa Sa'eed described as his sole weapon: "that sharp knife inside my skull, while within my breast was a cold, hard feeling." Tayeb Salih offered to the Arab novel a new language in which restraint and precision took precedence over exuberance. His prose moves with the cunning and inevitability of a great river searching for the sea.

—HISHAM MATAR

To Julie & Zainab

The *doum tree*
of *Wad Hamid*

دومـــة ود حـــامد

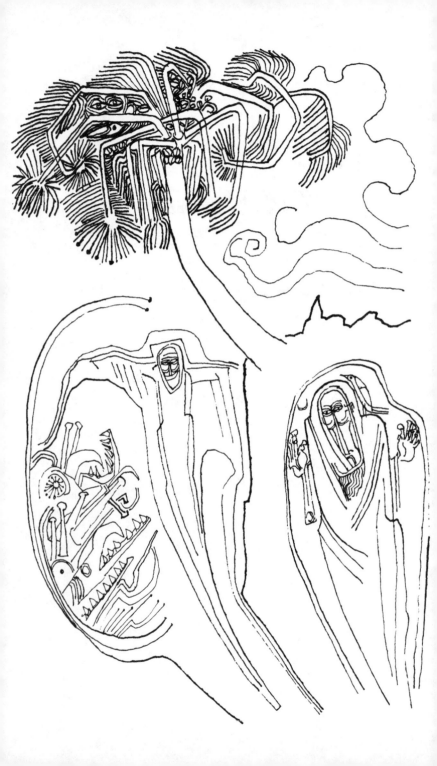

Were you to come to our village as a tourist, it is likely, my son, that you would not stay long. If it were in winter time, when the palm trees are pollinated, you would find that a dark cloud had descended over the village. This, my son, would not be dust, nor yet that mist which rises up after rainfall. It would be a swarm of those sand-flies which obstruct all paths to those who wish to enter our village. Maybe you have seen this pest before, but I swear that you have never seen this particular species. Take this gauze netting, my son, and put it over your head. While it won't protect you against these devils, it will at least help you to bear them. I remember a friend of my son's, a fellow student at school, whom my son invited to stay with us a year ago at this time of the year. His people come from the town. He stayed one night with us and got up next day, feverish, with a running nose and swollen face; he swore that he wouldn't spend another night with us.

If you were to come to us in summer you would find the horse-flies with us—enormous flies the size of young sheep, as we say. In comparison to these the sand-flies are a thousand times more bearable. They are savage flies, my son: they bite, sting, buzz, and whirr. They have a special love for man and no sooner smell him out than they attach themselves to him. Wave them off you, my son—God curse all sand-flies.

And were you to come at a time which was neither summer nor winter you would find nothing at all. No doubt, my son, you read the papers daily, listen to the radio, and go to the cinema once or twice a week. Should you become ill you have the right to be treated in hospital, and if you have a son he is entitled to receive education at a. school. I know, my son, that you hate dark streets and like to see electric light shining out into the night. I know, too, that you are not enamoured of walking and that riding donkeys gives you a bruise on your backside. Oh, I wish, my son, I wish—the asphalted roads of the towns—the modern means of transport—the fine comfortable buses. We have none of all this—we are people who live on what God sees fit to give us.

Tomorrow you will depart from our village, of this I am sure, and you will be right to do so. What have you to do with such hardship? We are thick-skinned people and in this we differ from others. We have become used to this hard life, in fact we like it, but we ask no one to subject himself to the difficulties of our life. Tomorrow you will depart, my son—I know that. Before you leave, though, let me show you one thing—something which, in a manner of speaking, we are proud of. In the towns you have museums, places in which the local history and the great deeds of the past are preserved. This thing that I want to show you can be said to be a museum. It is one thing we insist our visitors should see.

Once a preacher, sent by the government, came to us to stay for a month. He arrived at a time when the horse-flies had never been fatter. On the very first day the man's face swelled up. He bore this manfully and joined us in evening prayers on the second night, and after prayers he talked to us of the delights of the primitive life. On the third day he was down with malaria, he contracted dysentery, and his eyes were completely gummed up. I visited him at noon and found him prostrate in bed, with a boy standing at his head waving away the flies.

'O Sheikh,' I said to him, 'there is nothing in our village

to show you, though I would like you to see the doum tree of
Wad Hamid.' He didn't ask me what Wad Hamid's doum tree
was, but I presumed that he had heard of it, for who has not?
He raised his face which was like the lung of a slaughtered cow;
his eyes (as I said) were firmly closed; though I knew that
behind the lashes there lurked a certain bitterness.

'By God,' he said to me, 'if this were the doum tree of
Jandal, and you the Moslems who fought with Ali and
Mu'awiya, and I the arbitrator between you, holding your fate
in these two hands of mine, I would not stir an inch!' and he
spat upon the ground as though to curse me and turned his
face away. After that we heard that the Sheikh had cabled to
those who had sent him, saying: 'The horse-flies have eaten into
my neck, malaria has burnt up my skin, and dysentery has
lodged itself in my bowels. Come to my rescue, may God bless
you—these are people who are in no need of me or of any
other preacher.' And so the man departed and the government
sent us no preacher after him.

But, my son, our village actually witnessed many great men
of power and influence, people with names that rang through
the country like drums, whom we never even dreamed would
ever come here—they came, by God, in droves.

We have arrived. Have patience, my son; in a little while
there will be the noonday breeze to lighten the agony of this
pest upon your face.

Here it is: the doum tree of Wad Hamid. Look how it holds
its head aloft to the skies; look how its roots strike down into
the earth; look at its full, sturdy trunk, like the form of a
comely woman, at the branches on high resembling the mane of

a frolicsome steed! In the afternoon, when the sun is low, the doum tree casts its shadow from this high mound right across the river so that someone sitting on the far bank can rest in its shade. At dawn, when the sun rises, the shadow of the tree stretches across the cultivated land and houses right up to the cemetery. Don't you think it is like some mythical eagle spreading its wings over the village and everyone in it? Once the government, wanting to put through an agricultural scheme, decided to cut it down: they said that the best place for setting up the pump was where the doum tree stood. As you can see, the people of our village are concerned solely with their everyday needs and I cannot remember their ever having rebelled against anything. However, when they heard about cutting down the doum tree they all rose up as one man and barred the district commissioner's way. That was in the time of foreign rule. The flies assisted them too—the horse-flies. The man was surrounded by the clamouring people shouting that if the doum tree were cut down they would fight the government to the last man, while the flies played havoc with the man's face. As his papers were scattered in the water we heard him cry out: 'All right—doum tree stay—scheme no stay!' And so neither the pump nor the scheme came about and we kept our doum tree.

Let us go home, my son, for this is no time for talking in the open. This hour just before sunset is a time when the army of sand-flies becomes particularly active before going to sleep. At such a time no one who isn't well-accustomed to them and has become as thick-skinned as we are can bear their stings. Look at it, my son, look at the doum tree: lofty, proud, and haughty as though—as though it were some ancient idol.

Wherever you happen to be in the village you can see it; in fact, you can even see it from four villages away.

Tomorrow you will depart from our village, of that there is no doubt, the mementoes of the short walk we have taken visible upon your face, neck and hands. But before you leave I shall finish the story of the tree, the doum tree of Wad Hamid. Come in, my son, treat this house as your own.

You ask who planted the doum tree?

No one planted it, my son. Is the ground in which it grows arable land? Do you not see that it is stony and appreciably higher than the river bank, like the pedestal of a statue, while the river twists and turns below it like a sacred snake, one of the ancient gods of the Egyptians? My son, no one planted it. Drink your tea, for you must be in need of it after the trying experience you have undergone. Most probably it grew up by itself, though no one remembers having known it other than as you now find it. Our sons opened their eyes to find it commanding the village. And we, when we take ourselves back to childhood memories, to that dividing line beyond which you remember nothing, see in our minds a giant doum tree standing on a river bank; everything beyond it is as cryptic as talismans, like the boundary between day and night, like that fading light which is not the dawn but the light directly preceding the break of day. My son, do you find that you can follow what I say? Are you aware of this feeling I have within me but which I am powerless to express? Every new generation finds the doum tree as though it had been born at the time of their birth and would grow up with them. Go and sit with the people of this village and listen to them recounting their dreams. A man awakens from sleep and tells his neighbour how he found himself in a vast sandy tract of land, the sand as white as pure silver; how his feet sank in as he walked so that he could only draw them out again with difficulty; how he walked and walked until he was overcome with thirst and stricken with hunger, while the sands stretched endlessly around him; how he climbed a hill and on reaching the top espied a dense forest of doum trees with a single tall tree in the centre which in comparison with the others looked like a camel amid a herd of goats; how the man went down the hill to find that the earth seemed to be rolled up before him so that it was but a few steps before he found himself under the doum tree of Wad Hamid; how he then discovered a vessel containing milk, its surface still fresh with froth, and how the milk did not go down though he drank until he had quenched his thirst. At which his neighbour says to him, 'Rejoice at release from your troubles.'

You can also hear one of the women telling her friend: 'It was as though I were in a boat sailing through a channel in the sea, so narrow that I could stretch out my hands and touch the shore on either side. I found myself on the crest of a mountainous wave which carried me upwards till I was almost touching the clouds, then bore me down into a dark, bottomless pit. I began shouting in my fear, but my voice seemed to be trapped in my throat. Suddenly I found the channel opening out a little. I saw that on the two shores were black, leafless trees with thorns, the tips of which were like the heads of hawks. I saw the two shores closing in upon me and the trees seemed to be walking towards me. I was filled with terror and called out at the top of my voice, "O Wad Hamid!" As I looked I saw a man with a radiant face and a heavy white beard flowing down over his chest, dressed in spotless white and holding a string of amber prayer-beads. Placing his hand on my brow he said: "Be not afraid," and I was calmed. Then I found the shore opening up and the water flowing gently. I looked to my left and saw fields of ripe corn, water-wheels turning, and cattle grazing, and on the shore stood the doum tree of Wad Hamid. The boat came to rest under the tree and the man got out, tied up the boat, and stretched out his hand to me. He then struck me gently on the shoulder with the string of beads, picked up a doum fruit from the ground and put it in my hand. When I turned round he was no longer there.'

'That was Wad Hamid,' her friend then says to her, 'you will have an illness that will bring you to the brink of death, but you will recover. You must make an offering to Wad Hamid under the doum tree.'

So it is, my son, that there is not a man or woman, young or old, who dreams at night without seeing the doum tree of Wad Hamid at some point in the dream.

You ask me why it was called the doum tree of Wad Hamid and who Wad Hamid was. Be patient, my son—have another cup of tea.

At the beginning of home rule a civil servant came to inform us that the government was intending to set up a stopping-place for the steamer. He told us that the national government wished to help us and to see us progress, and his face was radiant with enthusiasm as he talked. But he could see that the faces around him expressed no reaction. My son, we are not people who travel very much, and when we wish to do so for some important matter such as registering land, or seeking advice about a matter of divorce, we take a morning's ride on our donkeys and then board the steamer from the neighbouring village. My son, we have grown accustomed to this, in fact it is precisely for this reason that we breed donkeys. It is little wonder, then, that the government official could see nothing in the people's faces to indicate that they were pleased with the news. His enthusiasm waned and, being at his wit's end, he began to fumble for words.

'Where will the stopping-place be?' someone asked him after a period of silence. The official replied that there was only one suitable place—where the doum tree stood. Had you that instant brought along a woman and had her stand among those men as naked as the day her mother bore her, they could not have been more astonished.

'The steamer usually passes here on a Wednesday,' one of the men quickly replied; 'if you made a stopping-place, then it would be here on Wednesday afternoon.' The official replied that the time fixed for the steamer to stop by their village would be four o'clock on Wednesday afternoon.

'But that is the time when we visit the tomb of Wad Hamid at the doum tree,' answered the man; 'when we take our women and children and make offerings. We do this every week.' The official laughed. 'Then change the day!' he replied. Had the official told these men at that moment that every one of them was a bastard, that would not have angered them more than this remark of his. They rose up as one man, bore down upon him, and would certainly have killed him if I had not intervened and snatched him from their clutches. I then put him on a donkey and told him to make good his escape.

And so it was that the steamer still does not stop here and that we still ride off on our donkeys for a whole morning and take the steamer from the neighbouring village when circumstances require us to travel. We content ourselves with the thought that we visit the tomb of Wad Hamid with our women and children and that we make offerings there every Wednesday as our fathers and fathers' fathers did before us.

Excuse me, my son, while I perform the sunset prayer—it is said that the sunset prayer is 'strange': if you don't catch it in time it eludes you. *God's pious servants—I declare that there is no god but God and I declare that Mohamed is His Servant and His Prophet—Peace be upon you and the mercy of God!*

Ah, ah. For a week this back of mine has been giving me pain. What do you think it is, my son? I know, though—it's just old age. Oh to be young! In my young days I would breakfast off half a sheep, drink the milk of five cows for supper, and be able to lift a sack of dates with one hand. He lies who says he ever beat me at wrestling. They used to call me 'the crocodile'. Once I swam the river, using my chest to push a boat loaded with wheat to the other shore—at night! On the shore were some men at work at their water-wheels, who threw down their clothes in terror and fled when they saw me pushing the boat towards them.

'Oh people,' I shouted at them, 'what's wrong, shame upon you! Don't you know me? I'm "the crocodile". By God, the devils themselves would be scared off by your ugly faces.'

My son, have you asked me what we do when we're ill?

I laugh because I know what's going on in your head. You townsfolk hurry to the hospital on the slightest pretext. If one of you hurts his finger you dash off to the doctor who puts a bandage on and you carry it in a sling for days; and even then it doesn't get better. Once I was working in the fields and something bit my finger—this little finger of mine. I jumped to my feet and looked around in the grass where I found a snake lurking. I swear to you it was longer than my arm. I took hold of it by the head and crushed it between two fingers, then bit into my finger, sucked out the blood, and took up a handful of dust and rubbed it on the bite.

But that was only a little thing. What do we do when faced with real illness?

This neighbour of ours, now. One day her neck swelled up and she was confined to bed for two months. One night she had a heavy fever, so at first dawn she rose from her bed and dragged herself along till she came—yes, my son, till she came to the doum tree of Wad Hamid. The woman told us what happened.

'I was under the doum tree,' she said, 'with hardly sufficient strength to stand up, and called out at the top of my voice: "O Wad Hamid, I have come to you to seek refuge and protection—I shall sleep here at your tomb and under your doum tree. Either you let me die or you restore me to life; I shall not leave here until one of these two things happens."

'And so I curled myself up in fear,' the woman continued with her story, 'and was soon overcome by sleep. While midway between wakefulness and sleep I suddenly heard

sounds of recitation from the Koran and a bright light, as sharp as a knife-edge, radiated out, joining up the two river banks, and I saw the doum tree prostrating itself in worship. My heart throbbed so violently that I thought it would leap up through my mouth. I saw a venerable old man with a white beard and wearing a spotless white robe come up to me, a smile on his face. He struck me on the head with his string of prayer-beads and called out: 'Arise.'

I swear that I got up I know not how and went home I know not how. I arrived back at dawn and woke up my husband, my son, and my daughters. I told my husband to light the fire and make tea. Then I ordered my daughters to give trilling cries of joy, and the whole village prostrated themselves before us. I swear that I have never again been afraid, nor yet ill.'

Yes, my son, we are people who have no experience of hospitals. In small matters such as the bites of scorpions, fever, sprains, and fractures, we take to our beds until we are cured. When in serious trouble we go to the doum tree.

Shall I tell you the story of Wad Hamid, my son, or would you like to sleep? Townsfolk don't go to sleep till late at night—I know that of them. We, though, go to sleep directly the birds are silent, the flies stop harrying the cattle, the leaves of the trees settle down, the hens spread their wings over their chicks, and the goats turn on their sides to chew the cud. We and our animals are alike: we rise in the morning when they rise and go to sleep when they sleep, our breathing and theirs following one and the same pattern.

My father, reporting what my grandfather had told him,

said: 'Wad Hamid, in times gone by, used to be the slave of a wicked man. He was one of God's holy saints but kept his faith to himself, not daring to pray openly lest his wicked master should kill him. When he could no longer bear his life with this infidel he called upon God to deliver him and a voice told him to spread his prayer-mat on the water and that when it stopped by the shore he should descend. The prayer-mat put him down at the place where the doum tree is now and which used to be waste land. And there he stayed alone, praying the whole day. At nightfall a man came to him with dishes of food, so he ate and continued his worship till dawn.'

All this happened before the village was built up. It is as though this village, with its inhabitants, its water-wheels and buildings, had become split off from the earth. Anyone who tells you he knows the history of its origin is a liar. Other places begin by being small and then grow larger, but this village of ours came into being at one bound. Its population neither increases nor decreases, while its appearance remains unchanged. And ever since our village has existed, so has the doum tree of Wad Hamid; and just as no one remembers how it originated and grew, so no one remembers how the doum tree came to grow in a patch of rocky ground by the river, standing above it like a sentinel.

When I took you to visit the tree, my son, do you remember the iron railing round it? Do you remember the marble plaque standing on a stone pedestal with 'The doum tree of Wad Hamid' written on it? Do you remember the doum tree with the gilded crescents above the tomb? They are the only new things about the village since God first planted it here, and

I shall now recount to you how they came into being.

When you leave us tomorrow—and you will certainly do so, swollen of face and inflamed of eye—it will be fitting if you do not curse us but rather think kindly of us and of the things that I have told you this night, for you may well find that your visit to us was not wholly bad.

You remember that some years ago we had Members of Parliament and political parties and a great deal of to-ing and fro-ing which we couldn't make head or tail of. The roads would sometimes cast down strangers at our very doors, just as the waves of the sea wash up strange weeds. Though not a single one of them prolonged his stay beyond one night, they would nevertheless bring us the news of the great fuss going on in the capital. One day they told us that the government which had driven out imperialism had been substituted by an even bigger and noisier government.

'And who has changed it?' we asked them, but received no answer. As for us, ever since we refused to allow the stopping-place to be set up at the doum tree no one has disturbed our tranquil existence. Two years passed without our knowing what form the government had taken, black or white. Its emissaries passed through our village without staying in it, while we thanked God that He had saved us the trouble of putting them up. So things went on till, four years ago, a new government came into power. As though this new authority wished to make us conscious of its presence, we awoke one day to find an official with an enormous hat and small head, in the company of two soldiers, measuring up and doing calculations at the doum tree. We asked them what it was about, to which they replied that the government wished to build a stopping-place for the steamer under the doum tree.

'But we have already given you our answer about that,' we told them. 'What makes you think we'll accept it now?'

'The government which gave in to you was a weak one,' they said, 'but the position has now changed.'

To cut a long story short, we took them by the scruffs of their necks, hurled them into the water, and went off to our work. It wasn't more than a week later when a group of soldiers came along commanded by the small-headed official with the large hat, shouting, 'Arrest that man, and that one, and that one,' until they'd taken off twenty of us, I among them. We spent a month in prison. Then one day the very soldiers who had put us there opened the prison gates. We asked them what it was all about but no one said anything. Outside the prison we found a great gathering of people; no sooner had we been spotted than there were shouts and cheering and we were embraced by some cleanly-dressed people, heavily scented and with gold watches gleaming on their wrists. They carried us off in a great procession, back to our own people. There we found an unbelievably immense gathering of people, carts, horses, and camels. We said to each other, 'The din and flurry of the capital has caught up with us.' They made us twenty men stand in a row and the people passed along it shaking us by the hand: the Prime Minister—the President of the Parliament—the President of the Senate—the member for such and such constituency—the member for such and such other constituency.

We looked at each other without understanding a thing of

what was going on around us except that our arms were aching with all the handshakes we had been receiving from those Presidents and Members of Parliament.

Then they took us off in a great mass to the place where the doum tree and the tomb stand. The Prime Minister laid the foundation stone for the monument you've seen, and for the dome you've seen, and for the railing you've seen. Like a tornado blowing up for a while and then passing over, so that mighty host disappeared as suddenly as it had come without spending a night in the village—no doubt because of the horse-flies which, that particular year, were as large and fat and buzzed and whirred as much as during the year the preacher came to us.

One of those strangers who were occasionally cast upon us in the village later told us the story of all this fuss and bother.

'The people,' he said, 'hadn't been happy about this government since it had come to power, for they knew that it had got there by bribing a number of the Members of Parliament. They therefore bided their time and waited for the right opportunities to present themselves, while the opposition looked around for something to spark things off. When the doum tree incident occurred and they marched you all off and slung you into prison, the newspapers took this up and the leader of the government which had resigned made a fiery speech in Parliament in which he said:

'To such tyranny has this government come that it has begun to interfere in the beliefs of the people, in those holy things held most sacred by them.' Then, taking a most imposing stance and in a voice choked with emotion, he said: 'Ask our worthy Prime Minister about the doum tree of Wad Hamid. Ask him how it was that he permitted himself to send his troops and henchmen to desecrate that pure and holy place!'

'The people took up the cry and throughout the country their hearts responded to the incident of the doum tree as to nothing before. Perhaps the reason is that in every village in this country there is some monument like the doum tree of Wad Hamid which people see in their dreams. After a month of fuss and shouting and inflamed feelings, fifty members of the government were forced to withdraw their support, their constituencies having warned them that unless they did so they would wash their hands of them. And so the government fell, the first government returned to power and the leading paper in the country wrote: "The doum tree of Wad Hamid has become the symbol of the nation's awakening."'

Since that day we have been unaware of the existence of the new government and not one of those great giants of men who visited us has put in an appearance; we thank God that He has spared us the trouble of having to shake them by the hand. Our life returned to what it had been: no water-pump, no agricultural scheme, no stopping-place for the steamer. But we kept our doum tree which casts its shadow over the southern bank in the afternoon and, in the morning, spreads its shadow over the fields and houses right up to the cemetery, with the river flowing below it like some sacred legendary snake. And our village has acquired a marble monument, an iron railing, and a dome with gilded crescents.

When the man had finished what he had to say he looked at

me with an enigmatic smile playing at the corners of his mouth like the faint flickerings of a lamp.

'And when,' I asked, 'will they set up the water-pump, and put through the agricultural scheme and the stopping-place for the steamer?'

He lowered his head and paused before answering me, 'When people go to sleep and don't see the doum tree in their dreams.'

'And when will that be?' I said.

'I mentioned to you that my son is in the town studying at school,' he replied. 'It wasn't I who put him there; he ran away and went there on his own, and it is my hope that he will stay where he is and not return. When my son's son passes out of school and the number of young men with souls foreign to our own increases, then perhaps the water-pump will be set up and the agricultural scheme put into being—maybe then the steamer will stop at our village—under the doum tree of Wad Hamid.'

'And do you think,' I said to him, 'that the doum tree will one day be cut down?' He looked at me for a long while as though wishing to project, through his tired, misty eyes, something which he was incapable of doing by word.

'There will not be the least necessity for cutting down the doum tree. There is not the slightest reason for the tomb to be removed. What all these people have overlooked is that there's plenty of room for all these things: the doum tree, the tomb, the water-pump, and the steamer's stopping-place.'

When he had been silent for a time he gave me a look which I don't know how to describe, though it stirred within me a feeling of sadness, sadness for some obscure thing which I was unable to define. Then he said: 'Tomorrow, without doubt, you will be leaving us. When you arrive at your destination, think well of us and judge us not too harshly.'

A handful
of dates

حفنـــة تـــمُر

I must have been very young at the time. While I don't remember exactly how old I was, I do remember that when people saw me with my grandfather they would pat me on the head and give my cheek a pinch—things they didn't do to my grandfather. The strange thing was that I never used to go out with my father, rather it was my grandfather who would take me with him wherever he went, except for the mornings when I would go to the mosque to learn the Koran. The mosque, the river and the fields—these were the landmarks in our life. While most of the children of my age grumbled at having to go to the mosque to learn the Koran, I used to love it. The reason was, no doubt, that I was quick at learning by heart and the Sheikh always asked me to stand up and recite the *Chapter of the Merciful* whenever we had visitors, who would pat me on my head and cheek just as people did when they saw me with my grandfather.

Yes, I used to love the mosque, and I loved the river too. Directly we finished our Koran reading in the morning I would throw down my wooden slate and dart off, quick as a genie, to my mother, hurriedly swallow down my breakfast, and run off for a plunge in the river. When tired of swimming about I would sit on the bank and gaze at the strip of water that wound away eastwards and hid behind a thick wood of acacia trees. I loved to give rein to my imagination and picture to myself a tribe of giants living behind that wood, a people tall and thin with white beards and sharp noses, like my grandfather. Before my grandfather ever replied to my many questions he would rub the tip of his nose with his forefinger; as for his beard, it was soft and luxuriant and as white as cotton-wool—never in my life have I seen anything of a purer whiteness or greater beauty. My grandfather must also have been extremely tall, for I never saw anyone in the whole area address him without having to look up at him, nor did I see him enter a house without having to bend so low that I was put in mind of the way the river wound round behind the wood of acacia trees. I loved him and would imagine myself, when I grew to be a man, tall and slender like him, walking along with great strides.

I believe I was his favourite grandchild: no wonder, for my cousins were a stupid bunch and I—so they say—was an intelligent child. I used to know when my grandfather wanted me to laugh, when to be silent; also I would remember the times for his prayers and would bring him his prayer-rug and fill the ewer for his ablutions without his having to ask me. When he had nothing else to do he enjoyed listening to me reciting to him from the Koran in a lilting voice, and I could tell from his face that he was moved.

One day I asked him about our neighbour Masood. I said to my grandfather: 'I fancy you don't like our neighbour Masood?'

To which he answered, having rubbed the tip of his nose: 'He's an indolent man and I don't like such people.'

I said to him: 'What's an indolent man?'

My grandfather lowered his head for a moment, then looking across at the wide expanse of field, he said: 'Do you see it stretching out from the edge of the desert up to the Nile bank? A hundred feddans. Do you see all those date palms?

And those trees—*sant*, acacia, and *sayal*? All this fell into Masood's lap, was inherited by him from his father.'

Taking advantage of the silence that had descended upon my grandfather, I turned my gaze from him to the vast area defined by his words. 'I don't care,' I told myself, 'who owns those date palms, those trees or this black, cracked earth—all I know is that it's the arena for my dreams and my playground.'

My grandfather then continued: 'Yes, my boy, forty years ago all this belonged to Masood—two-thirds of it is now mine.'

This was news to me for I had imagined that the land had belonged to my grandfather ever since God's Creation.

'I didn't own a single feddan when I first set foot in this village. Masood was then the owner of all these riches. The position has changed now, though, and I think that before Allah calls me to Him I shall have bought the remaining third as well.'

I do not know why it was I felt fear at my grandfather's words—and pity for our neighbour Masood. How I wished my grandfather wouldn't do what he'd said! I remembered Masood's singing, his beautiful voice and powerful laugh that resembled the gurgling of water. My grandfather never used to laugh.

I asked my grandfather why Masood had sold his land.

'Women,' and from the way my grandfather pronounced the word I felt that 'women' was something terrible. 'Masood, my boy, was a much-married man. Each time he married he sold me a feddan or two.' I made the quick calculation that Masood must have married some ninety women. Then I remembered his three wives, his shabby appearance, his lame donkey and its dilapidated saddle, his *galabia* with the torn sleeves. I had all but rid my mind of the thoughts that jostled in it when I saw the man approaching us, and my grandfather and I exchanged glances.

'We'll be harvesting the dates today,' said Masood. 'Don't you want to be there?'

I felt, though, that he did not really want my grandfather to attend. My grandfather, however, jumped to his feet and I saw that his eyes sparkled momentarily with an intense brightness. He pulled me by the hand and we went off to the harvesting of Masood's dates.

Someone brought my grandfather a stool covered with an ox-hide, while I remained standing. There was a vast number of people there, but though I knew them all, I found myself for some reason, watching Masood: aloof from that great gathering of people he stood as though it were no concern of his, despite the fact that the date palms to be harvested were his own. Sometimes his attention would be caught by the sound of a huge clump of dates crashing down from on high. Once he shouted up at the boy perched on the very summit of the date palm who had begun hacking at a clump with his long, sharp sickle: 'Be careful you don't cut the heart of the palm.'

No one paid any attention to what he said and the boy seated at the very summit of the date palm continued, quickly and energetically, to work away at the branch with his sickle till the clump of dates began to drop like something descending from the heavens.

I, however, had begun to think about Masood's phrase 'the

heart of the palm.' I pictured the palm tree as something with feeling, something possessed of a heart that throbbed. I remembered Masood's remark to me when he had once seen me playing about with the branch of a young palm tree: 'Palm trees, my boy, like humans, experience joy and suffering.' And I had felt an inward and unreasoned embarrassment.

When I again looked at the expanse of ground stretching before me I saw my young companions swarming like ants around the trunks of the palm trees, gathering up dates and eating most of them. The dates were collected into high mounds. I saw people coming along and weighing them into measuring bins and pouring them into sacks, of which I counted thirty. The crowd of people broke up, except for Hussein the merchant, Mousa the owner of the field next to ours on the east, and two men I'd never seen before.

I heard a low whistling sound and saw that my grandfather had fallen asleep. Then I noticed that Masood had not changed his stance, except that he had placed a stalk in his mouth and was munching at it like someone surfeited with food who doesn't know what to do with the mouthful he still has.

Suddenly my grandfather woke up, jumped to his feet and walked towards the sacks of dates. He was followed by Hussein the merchant, Mousa the owner of the field next to ours, and the two strangers. I glanced at Masood and saw that he was making his way towards us with extreme slowness, like a man who wants to retreat but whose feet insist on going forward. They formed a circle round the sacks of dates and began examining them, some taking a date or two to eat. My grandfather gave me a fistful, which I began munching. I saw Masood filling the palms of both hands with dates and bringing them up close to his nose, then returning them.

Then I saw them dividing up the sacks between them. Hussein the merchant took ten; each of the strangers took five. Mousa the owner of the field next to ours on the eastern side took five, and my grandfather took five. Understanding nothing, I looked at Masood and saw that his eyes were darting about to left and right like two mice that have lost their way home.

'You're still fifty pounds in debt to me,' said my grandfather to Masood. 'We'll talk about it later.'

Hussein called his assistants and they brought along donkeys, the two strangers produced camels, and the sacks of dates were loaded on to them. One of the donkeys let out a braying which set the camels frothing at the mouth and complaining noisily. I felt myself drawing close to Masood, felt my hand stretch out towards him as though I wanted to touch the hem of his garment. I heard him make a noise in his throat like the rasping of a lamb being slaughtered. For some unknown reason, I experienced a sharp sensation of pain in my chest.

I ran off into the distance. Hearing my grandfather call after me, I hesitated a little, then continued on my way. I felt at that moment that I hated him. Quickening my pace, it was as though I carried within me a secret I wanted to rid myself of. I reached the river bank near the bend it made behind the wood of acacia trees. Then, without knowing why, I put my finger into my throat and spewed up the dates I'd eaten.

The wedding
of Zein

عــــــرسُ الـــــــزين

'Have you heard the news? Zein is getting married,' said Haleema, the seller of milk, to Amna, who had as usual called before sunrise, as she measured her out a piastre's worth.

The jug all but fell from Amna's hands and Haleema, profiting by her preoccupation, gave her short measure.

At noon the courtyard of the Intermediate School was quiet and deserted, the students having gone to their classes. From afar there appeared a young boy hurrying along breathlessly, the end of his outer garment tucked under his arm, till he came to a stop in front of the door of 'the second year,' the Headmaster's form.

'You ass of a boy, what's made you so late?'

A look of cunning flashed momentarily in Tureifi's eyes,

'Sir, have you heard the news?'

'News about what, you animal of a boy?'

The Headmaster's anger, however, did not shake the boy's composure. Checking his laughter, he said: 'They're marrying off Zein the day after tomorrow.'

The Headmaster's lower jaw dropped in astonishment and Tureifi escaped punishment.

And in the market Abdul Samad advanced towards Sheikh Ali's shop, his face flushed, leaving it in no doubt that he was in an angry frame of mind. There was a debt owing to him from Sheikh Ali, the tobacco dealer, which the latter had put off paying for a whole month. He was determined to have it settled that very day by hook or by crook.

'Ali, do you really think you'll do me out of my money, or what is it you've got in mind?'

'Hajj Abdul Samad, just put your trust in God and sit down and have a cup of coffee with us.'

'To hell with your coffee. Get up and open this safe of yours and give me my money. If you're determined not to pay, just say so.'

Sheikh Ali spat the quid of tobacco from his mouth.

'Come along and sit down and I'll tell you a bit of news.'

'I've not got the time, neither for you nor for your bit of news. I know well enough that you're trying to fool me and talk me out of my money.'

'I swear your money's here safe and sound. Come along and sit down and I'll tell you the story of Zein's marriage.'

'Whose marriage did you say?'

'Zein's marriage.'

Abdul Samad seated himself and, placing both hands on top of his head, remained silent for a while. Sheikh Ali regarded him, elated at the effect he had produced. Eventually Abdul Samad found his tongue.

'Ah, there's no god but God and Mohammed is the Prophet of God. By the Prophet himself, Sheikh Ali, what sort of story's that?'

Abdul Samad did not settle his debt that day.

By midday every one's tongue was wagging with the news. Zein himself was at the well in the centre of the village, filling the women's pitchers for them and indulging in his usual antics.

The children gathered round him and began chanting, 'Zein's getting married—Zein's getting married,' while he hurled stones at them, tugged at a girl's dress, prodded a woman in her middle, or pinched another's thigh; children laughed, the women shrieked and laughed, and above all this laughter could be heard the laugh that had become part of the village ever since Zein was born.

At first, as is well known, children meet life with screams. With Zein, however, it is recounted—and the authorities for this are his mother and the women who attended his birth— that no sooner did he come into this world than he burst out laughing. And so it was throughout his life.

He had grown up with only two teeth in his mouth, one in his upper jaw and one in the lower. His mother, though, says that his mouth was once filled with pearly white teeth, but that when he was six she took him one day to visit some relatives of hers; at sunset, passing by a deserted ruin rumoured to be haunted, Zein had suddenly become nailed to the ground and had begun shivering as with a fever. Then he let out a scream. After that he took to his bed for several days, and on recovering from his illness it was found that all his teeth had fallen out—except for one in his upper jaw and one in the lower.

Zein had an elongated face with prominent bones to his cheeks, his jaw, and under the eyes. His forehead was rounded and jutted out; his eyes were small and permanently bloodshot, their sockets deeply set in his face like two caverns. His face was completely hairless, with neither eyebrows nor eyelashes, and on attaining manhood no hair had sprouted on his chin or upper lip.

This face of his was supported by a long neck (among the nicknames given to Zein by the children was 'the giraffe') which stood on two powerful shoulders that straddled the rest of the body, forming a triangle. The two long arms were like those of a monkey, the hands coarse with extended fingers ending in long, sharp nails (Zein never pared them). His chest was concave, his back slightly hunched, while his legs were long and spindly like those of a crane. His feet were splayed and bore the traces of ancient scars (Zein disliked wearing shoes), and he remembered the story behind each one of them.

For example, the story of a long scar on his right foot extending from the back of the ankle to the opening between the first and second toes, Zein recounted as follows: 'Now this scar, men, has a story to it.'

And Mahjoub would egg him on with the words, 'And what story would this be, you good-for-nothing? Did you go off to steal and they give you a hiding with a thorn tree branch?'

This would have a splendid effect on Zein, who would fall over backwards, legs raised high in the air and hands beating the ground, while continuing to give vent to that strange and singular laughter that resembled a donkey's braying. Infected by him, everyone else would burst into loud reverberating guffaws. Collecting himself, Zein would wipe the tears away with his cuff and say: 'Yea—yea—so I did go off to steal—'

Mahjoub would again egg him on: 'And what did you go off to steal, you scoundrel? Perhaps you said to yourself

you'd look around for something to eat.' And Zein, wiping
his hands across his face, would once again break into laughter,
and those present would presume that he had come by that
particular scar entering some house to steal food, for he was
well-known for his insatiable greed. At wedding feasts, when
the trays of food were brought in and the people formed
themselves into circles around them, each group tried to avoid
having Zein sitting with them, as he would dispose of everything in the dish in a flash, leaving nothing for anyone else.

'Do you remember what you did at Sa'eed's wedding?'
Abdul Hafeez said to him.

'Certainly I do,' Zein answered with a guffaw. 'By God,
I would have eaten up the lot right down to the last little bit
if Isma'il's son, God damn him, hadn't caught me.' Zein had
been entrusted with transporting the food at Sa'eed's wedding
and had walked back and forth between the *diwan*, where the
men were congregated, and the kitchen at the back of the house,
where the women were doing the cooking. On the way from
the kitchen to the *diwan* Zein dawdled along, eating the choic-
est bits from the dish he was carrying, so that on arrival it was
all but empty. He did this three times before Ahmed Isma'il
noticed what was happening and followed him. Halfway to
the *diwan* Zein stopped and lifted the lid off a dish filled with
fried chicken. No sooner had he taken hold of a chicken and
brought it to his mouth than Ahmed Isma'il pounced upon him
and gave him a sound beating.

'Come along,' Mahjoub again asked him, 'why don't you tell
us what you went off to steal, you rogue?'

When Zein noticed that the people around him were all agog

to hear, he sat up straight, placed his arms between his knees and said: 'Last summer, at the time of the harvesting of the millet, I was kept late at the water-wheel. The moon was atwinkle as I tossed my shawl across my shoulder and came up homewards. I tell you, when I reached the patch of sand by the edge of the village I heard the sounds of joyful ululation.'

'Yes, that's quite right,' Mahjoub interrupted him. 'That was Bakri's wedding.'

Zein continued: 'And so I told myself I'd go along and see what it was all about. Now it seems that the Talha people were having a wedding and when I got there I found that things had really hotted up—a proper hullabaloo with drums and ululations. The first thing I did was to go off and look to see if I could find something to eat—'

The gathering burst into laughter, for it was what they had expected. 'The women in the kitchen gave me some bits of meat to eat and something bitter to drink.'

'That must have been arak, you good-for-nothing,' said Mahjoub.

'No, it wasn't arak,' said Zein. 'Do you think I don't know what arak is? I'm telling you, man, this thing I drank really flew to my head. Afterwards I slipped out of the kitchen and went into a room where I found a group of women and the smell of perfumes and scented ointments. May I divorce if the very smell didn't intoxicate me.'

Abdul Hafeez laughed. 'And where is the woman you'd be divorcing?'

Zein paid no attention to this but continued enthusiastically with the story. 'And right in the middle I found the bride—a sweet little chit of a girl, all beautiful-smelling from the smoke bath and finely dressed.' Zein became silent at this point and turned his small eyes on the faces of those present, his mouth agape, his two teeth jutting out.

Mahjoub, unable to contain himself, egged him on to complete the story. 'And what did you do then?'

'Then—I jumped on the bride.' Having said which he leapt up like a frog. Everyone broke into an uproar and Zein exploded into laughter and threw himself down on his stomach, kicking up his legs in the air. Then he turned over on to his back and said, still choking with laughter: 'I took hold of the little girl and bit her on the mouth.'

Mahjoub was so shocked that he muttered 'There is no god but God and Mohammed is His Prophet,' and asked His forgiveness for having even heard something so terrible.

'I tell you, the women raised hell, the whole house was in an uproar, and the young bride began screaming. All of a sudden I found that somebody'd struck me in the ankle with a knife. I tell you, I started running and didn't stop till I arrived back home.' Suddenly Zein sat upright, the expression on his face wholly serious and, directing his words at Mahjoub, said: 'Listen, are you going to marry your daughter Alawiyya to me or aren't you?'

'I promise the girl to you—right now before all these people here,' Mahjoub answered him in all seriousness, as though meaning what he said. 'After you've reaped your wheat and gathered up your dates and sold them and brought the money, we'll make the wedding celebration.'

This promise satisfied Zein. For a while he remained silent

with pursed lips, as though he had started to think about his future life with Alawiyya and the responsibility of taking on the cares of a wife and children. 'That's it, then,' he said. 'Bear witness, brothers—this man has given his word and he can't come along denying it tomorrow or the day after.' All those present—Ahmed Isma'il, Taher Rawwasi, Abdul Hafeez, Hamad Wad Rayyes, and Sa'eed the shopkeeper—stated that they were witnesses to the promise made by Mahjoub and that the marriage would, God permitting, take place.

The story of Zein's love for Alawiyya the daughter of Mahjoub is the latest of his romances. After a month or two he will tire of it and begin some new romance. For the present, though, he is completely taken up with her and she is ever-present in his mind. In the middle of the day you find him in the field, bent over his hoe, his face pouring with sweat, when he suddenly stops digging and cries out at the top of his voice, 'I am slain by love in the courtyard of Mahjoub.' In neighbouring fields tens of people momentarily stop digging as they listen to Zein's cry. While the young men laugh, some of the older men, who are occasionally irritated by Zein's tomfoolery, mumble with annoyance, 'What's that crazy boy gabbling about now?' When at sunset work in the field comes to an end and the people take themselves off to their houses, Zein walks home from the field amidst a large crowd of young men, boys and girls, all laughing merrily around him, as he struts about among them, striking a young man on the shoulder, pinching a girl's cheek, and making leaps into the air. Whenever he sees an acacia bush along the way he jumps over it and from time to time lets out

shrieks at the top of his voice that resound through the village
on which the sun has set. 'Hear ye, you people of the village,
O kinsfolk, I am slain by love in the courtyard of Mahjoub.'

Zein was first slain by love when he had still not attained
manhood. He was thirteen or fourteen at the time and was
as thin and emaciated as a dried-up stalk. Whatever people
might say about Zein they acknowledged his impeccable taste,
for he fell in love with none but the most beautiful girls, the
best mannered and most pleasant of speech. Azza, daughter of
the Omda, was fifteen years old and her beauty had suddenly
unfolded in the same way as a young palm tree flourishes when,
after thirsting, it is given water. Her skin was as gold as a
field of wheat just before harvesting; her eyes were wide and
black in a face of limpid beauty, her features delicate; her eye-
lashes were long and when she slowly raised them one would
experience a quickening of the heart. Zein was the first to
draw the attention of the young men of the village to Azza's
beauty. One day he suddenly raised his voice whilst amid a
great gathering of men brought together by the Omda for the
cultivation of his field, raised his hoarse, piercing voice as
does the cock at the break of dawn: 'Hear ye, O people of
the village, O kinsfolk, Azza the Omda's daughter has slain
herself a man. Zein is slain in the courtyard of the Omda.' The
people were taken aback by such daring and the Omda turned
round sharply towards Zein, instinctve anger rising within
him. Suddenly, as though everyone had at one and the same
instant become conscious of the laughable disparity between
Zein's appearance, standing there as though he were a dried-up

goat's skin, and between Azza the Omda's daughter, they all burst out laughing at one accord.

The anger died in the breast of the Omda, who was seated on a chair in the shade of a palm tree, red of eye and dusty of moustache, as he spurred the people on to work. He was a serious, awe-inspiring man who seldom laughed; however, on this occasion he gave a harsh explosive laugh at Zein's words. 'Zein,' he shouted out at him, 'if you go on working hard till evening we'll give you Azza in marriage,' and once again the people laughed, in deference to the Omda. Zein, however, remained silent, his face serious and preoccupied, unconscious of the increasing strength and frequency of the strokes of his hoe in the ground.

After that a month elapsed with Zein talking of nothing but his love for Azza and her father's promise that he would marry her. The Omda knew how to exploit Zein's emotions and gave him any number of arduous tasks which would have defeated the jinn themselves. So Zein the Lover would be seen bearing a yoke with tins of water on his back at high noon when the very stones groaned with the heat, hurrying to and fro as he watered the Omda's garden; or he would be found wielding an axe larger than himself and cutting down a tree or chopping up wood; or you'd come upon him earnestly engaged in gathering fodder for the Omda's donkeys, horses, and calves. And when, once a week, Azza smiled at him the whole world could hardly contain him for joy. Not a month passed, though, before it became known in the village that Azza had become engaged to her cousin, who worked as a Medical Assistant at Abu Usher.

Without fuss, without saying a word, Zein started on a
new romance. One day the village awoke to his cries of: 'I am
slain among the people of the Koz.' His 'Laila' this time was
a young girl from among the bedouin who lived along the Nile
in the north of the Sudan and came down from the lands of
the Kababeesh and the Dar Hamar, and from the encampments
of the Hawaweer and the Mereisab in Kordofan. At certain
seasons water became scarce in their lands and they would
journey down the Nile with their camels and sheep in search of
watering for them. Sometimes years of drought, when the sky
withheld rain, would bring them down and they would arrive
in droves at the watering-places in the lands of the Shaigiya
and the Bideeriya who lived along the Nile. Most of them
remained only until things got better, when they would return
whence they had come, though some of them, taking a liking
to the settled life in the Nile valley, stayed on. The bedouin
of the Koz were one such group. They continued to pitch their
tents on the edge of the cultivated land, where they pastured
their sheep and sold the milk, collected wood for fuel, and
hired themselves out at low rates in the date-harvesting season.
They did not intermarry with the local inhabitants, considering
themselves to be pure Arabs. The village people, however,
regarded them as uncouth bedouin.

Zein, though, broke down this barrier. Always on the move,
spending all day long wandering through the area from end
to end, his feet one day led him for no particular reason to the
people of the Koz. He was roaming round the tents as though
looking for something he'd lost, when a girl appeared and
Zein, struck by her beauty, was rooted to the spot. The girl

had heard of him, for his fame had reached even as far as the bedouin of the Koz, so she laughed and said jokingly, 'Zein, will you marry me?' He was speechless for a while—in the thrall of the girl's beauty, he was now made spellbound by the magic of her words. Then and there he called out at the top of his voice, 'O people, she has slain me.'

Many heads craned out from the doors of the houses and from between the flaps of tents. The girl's mother called out, 'Haleema, what are you up to with that dervish?' And the girl's brothers rushed at Zein, who took to flight. But Haleema, the belle of the Koz, thereafter became the object of an infatuation that did not leave him till she was married. People got to hear about her and many of the wealthy men of the village, the eligible youths and notables, came to ask for her in marriage from her father. In the end she was married to the son of the Cadi.

The marriage of the Omda's daughter and that of Haleema were a turning-point in Zein's life, for the mothers of young girls woke up to his importance as a trumpet by which attention was drawn to their daughters. In a conservative society where girls are hidden away from young men, Zein became an emissary for Love, transporting its sweet fragrance from place to place. Love, first of all, would strike at his heart, then would be quickly transferred to the heart of another—just as though Zein were a broker, a salesman, or a postman. With his small mouse-like eyes lurking in their sunken sockets, Zein would look at a beautiful girl and would be overcome by something that was perhaps love. His innocent heart having succumbed to this love, his thin legs would carry him to the far corners of the village, running hither and thither like a bitch that has lost her pups, his tongue continually singing the girl's praises and calling out her name, so that ears were soon cocked and eyes on the look-out. Soon, too, some handsome young man's hand would stretch out to take that of the young girl. And when the wedding took place, if you looked around for Zein, you'd find him either working away at filling pitchers and large ewers with water, or standing bare-chested, axe in hand, in the middle of a courtyard cutting up firewood, or exchanging good-natured banter with the women in the kitchen, while from time to time they fed him with tit-bits and he'd burst out into that laugh of his, so like a donkey's braying. And then would begin another romance, and from each romance Zein would emerge unscathed and, to all appearances, unchanged: his laugh unaltered, his tomfoolery in no wise lessened, and his legs never weary of bearing his body to the outlying parts of the village.

Years of abundance replete with love were experienced by Zein. The young girls' mothers went out of their way to gain his affection, tempting him into their houses where they'd give him food to eat and tea and coffee to drink. On entering, a seat of honour would be spread out for him and breakfast or lunch served up in the best crockery, after which mint tea would be brought if it happened to be morning, or strong tea with milk if afternoon; after the tea he'd be served coffee with cinammon, cardamom, and ginger, be it morning or after-noon. No sooner did the women hear that Zein was in a nearby house than they'd flock to him, for they were amused by his raillery. Mothers would urge their daughters to go along and greet him, and lucky the one that gained a place in his heart and whose name was upon his lips when he went out, for such a girl was guaranteed a husband within a month or two. Perhaps Zein instinctively became aware of the importance of his new status and so began to play 'hard to get' with the girls' mothers and would show hesitation before accepting an invitation to breakfast or lunch. Yet with all this, there was one girl in the district about whom Zein did not speak and with whom he never played the fool. She was a girl who would observe him from afar with beautiful, sullen eyes and whenever he saw her approaching he would fall silent and leave off his raillery and bufoonery. If he spotted her far off he would flee from her presence, leaving the road to her.

Zein's mother put it about that her son was one of God's saints, and this belief was strengthened by Zein's friendship with Haneen. Haneen was a pious man wholly dedicated to his religious devotions who, having stayed six months in the village praying and fasting, would then take up his pitcher and prayer-rug and wander about up in the desert, disappearing for six months and then returning. No one knew where he went, though people related strange stories concerning him, one swearing that he had seen him in Merowi at a particular time, while another swore he'd caught sight of him in Karma at that very same time, though a distance of six days' journey separates the two places. People stated that Haneen would meet up with a group of those itinerant holy men who wander about devoting themselves to the service of God. Haneen seldom talked to any of the villagers, and if asked where he went to for six months of the year would make no reply. No one knew what he ate or drank, for he carried no provisions on his long journeys. But there was in the village one person with whom Haneen was on friendly terms: Zein. When meeting him upon the road, he would embrace him, kiss him on the head and call him 'The blessed one of God'. Zein, too, on seeing Haneen approach would leave off his horse-play and idle talk and would hasten up to embrace him. Haneen would not partake of food in any house but Zein's: off Zein would go to his mother and ask her to prepare them lunch, tea or coffee, and there Zein and Haneen would stay together for hours laughing and talking. The people of the village tried to learn from Zein the secret of the friendship between him and Haneen, but he would never say more than the words 'Haneen is a man blessed of God'.

Zein had numerous friendships of this sort with persons whom the villagers regarded as abnormal, such as Deaf Ashmana, Mousa the Lame, and Bekheit who was born deformed with no upper lip and a paralysed left side. Zein was fond of such people; thus, if he were to see Ashmana approaching from the field bearing a heavy load of firewood on her head, he would carry it for her with a playful smile. So afraid of people was she that if she came face to face with anyone, man or woman, she became utterly panic-stricken, just as though they were wild beasts. Yet she enjoyed Zein's company and would give him her sad, almost soundless laugh that resembled the clucking of hens. And then there was Mousa whom people called not by name but 'the Lame One', a man advanced in years, the mere sight of whom was enough to rend one's heart because of the great effort he had to make to walk, a man for whom life was an irksome and arduous road. He had been the slave of a well-to-do man in the village and when the government gave the slaves their freedom, Mousa had elected to stay on with his master, who had shown him great kindness, treating him like a son. At death the master's wealth had devolved upon a good-for-nothing son, who had dissipated it and driven Mousa out. Overtaken by old age, Mousa had found himself destitute, without a family or anyone to look after him. He therefore lived on the fringe of life in the village, just like the old stray dogs that howled in the waste plots of land at night and, harassed by boys, spent their days scavenging hither and thither for food. Zein, taking pity on the man, had built him a house of palm branches and provided him with a nanny goat in milk. In the morning he would go to enquire how he was and after sunset would come with his garment bulging with dates and other sorts of food, which he would lay before him. Occasionally he would bring along an ounce of tea, a pound of sugar, or a little coffee. If you asked Mousa about the friendship that existed between him and Zein he would say to you, his eyes brimming over with tears, 'Zein—Zein's a good fellow'.

The people of the village, seeing these acts of Zein's, would be even more amazed; perhaps he was the legendary Leader, the Prophet of God, perhaps an angel sent down by God in lowly human form in order to remind His worshippers that a great heart may yet beat even in one of concave breast and ridiculous manner such as Zein. Some would say: 'He places His strength in the weakest of His creatures'. And all the while Zein's voice would continue to call out 'O kinsfolk, O people of the village, I am slain', and this other picture of Zein would

be destroyed and replaced by the picture of him to which people
were accustomed and which they preferred. And all the while
there was a young girl in the community, of sweet dignified
countenance and flashing eyes, who watched Zein at his horse-
play and raillery. One day, finding him amidst a group of
women, joking with them in his usual way, she rebuked him
with the words, 'Why don't you give up this nonsensical chatter
and go off and get on with your work?' And she glared at the
women with her beautiful eyes. Zein stopped laughing and
lowered his head in shame. He then slunk out from among the
women and went his way.

Amna did not believe her ears. She asked Haleema, the seller
of milk, for the tenth time: 'Who did you say the lad was
getting married to?' and for the tenth time Haleema said:
'Ni'ma'. Impossible. The girl had surely gone out of her mind.
Ni'ma to marry Zein? Amazement mingled with anger in
Amna's breast, for she remembered clearly that day two
months ago when, swallowing her pride and plucking up her
courage, she had gone to Ni'ma's mother. She had previously
sworn not to speak to Saadiyya ever again, for when Amna's
own mother had died all the village women had come to pay
their condolences with the exception of Saadiyya. Amna did
not concern herself with the fact that Saadiyya had been away
from the village at the time when her mother died, having been
ill in hospital at Merowi, where she had been confined to bed
for a whole month. When she had returned from Merowi all
the women had come to enquire after her health with the
exception of Amna. The women were divided into two groups:

one held that Saadiyya was in the wrong and argued that duty decreed that it was she who should have begun by visiting Amna, death being of more moment than illness; the other group of women took Saadiyya's side and said that Amna's mother had in any case reached the age of decrepitude and that the living were more important than the dead. The situation grew increasingly involved as each of the two women stuck to her opinion. Thus Amna no longer spoke to Saadiyya, or Saadiyya to Amna.

This went on until two months back when Amna's son insisted that she go and ask on his behalf for Ni'ma's hand in marriage. So the woman swallowed her pride, plucked up her courage, and went to Saadiyya's house late in the morning when the coffee was bubbling over the fire and the cups and sugar and things were laid out on the table. Saadiyya received her off-handedly and coldly asked her if she'd have some coffee. When Amna refused, Saadiyya said nothing more and made no attempt to press her. She did not say to her: 'May the Prophet himself make you change your mind. God guide you, come along and drink some coffee'. She had said not one sentence more. It had taken a lot of courage from Amna to talk to Saadiyya on the subject of her son Ahmed and Ni'ma, Saadiyya's daughter. Calming down, she had swallowed hard and said in a quavering voice, while inwardly cursing her son who had exposed her to all this humiliation: 'Saadiyya, sister mine, I swore that not even a matter of life and death would ever bring me again to you, because you of all people had refused to come and offer me condolences on my mother's death. Yet even so the true Moslem is indulgent, and thus, sister, I forgive you. The point of my coming to you now—the thing that's brought me along—it's my son Ahmed—Ahmed's father and I would like to have Ni'ma for Ahmed'. When she had finished what she had to say, her tongue felt like a piece of wood in her mouth and her throat had contracted. She coughed nervously twice and her hands trembled.

Saadiyya said nothing. If she had uttered but one single word, Amna would have been put slightly at ease. Saadiyya always made her feel she was of lesser significance than herself; she was a beautiful woman of noble features, and when you looked at her serene and dignified face you were made aware of the wealth of her seven brothers, the vast properties of her father, and the countless date palms, trees, cows and livestock that were owned by her husband. This woman had three sons who had studied at school and worked for the government, also a beautiful daughter who was held in high regard by people and who was much sought after by the young men. This woman, who was over forty and looked like a young virgin girl, this woman of few words, why did she not say something? At last Saadiyya raised her long eye-lashes and gave Amna a look she did not understand: it contained neither anger nor malice, neither reproach nor affection. In her calm voice which neither trembled nor was raised, she said, 'God's will be done. Naturally the decision lies with the girl's father. When he comes we'll speak to him'.

Amna remembered all this, she remembered too how they had later refused, giving as their excuse the fact that Ni'ma was still a minor and not of marriageable age. And here they were marrying her to this boorish dolt of a man—Zein of all people. Amna felt that the affair was an intentional affront directed against her personally. Haleema, the seller of milk, became alarmed as she watched Amna's eyes widening in anger. Thinking that Amna had realised she had adulterated the milk, she poured out some more and said to her, 'Just a little extra to put you in a good mood.'

The years come and go, year follows year. The Nile's breast, like that of a man in anger, swells up, and the water flows over its banks, covering the cultivated land until it reaches the base of the houses at the fringe of the desert. The frogs croak at night, and from the north there blows a humid breeze bringing with it a smell that is a mixture of the perfume of the flower of the *talh* acacia tree and the smell of wet fire-wood, the smell of thirsting, fertile land when it is given water, and the smell of dead fish thrown up by the waves on to the sands. On moonlit nights, when the moon's face is rounded, the water turns into an enormous illuminated mirror over whose surface move the shadows of date palms and the branches of trees. The water carries sounds great distances; thus if a wedding party is being held two miles away, the ululations, the beating of drums, and the strains of the *tunbours* and *mizmars*, are heard as though right alongside your house. The Nile draws a deep breath and one day awakes from sleep and lo! its breast has sunk down and the water has drawn away from the sides, settling down into one large water-course that stretches eastwards and westwards—from it the sun rises in the mornings and into it it plunges at nightfall. As you look across you see the land extending away, smooth and sated; land on which the water has left shapely, polished tracks in

its flight to its natural course. Now the smell of the earth fills
your nostrils; it puts you in mind of the smell of the date palms
when they are ready for pollination. The land is motionless and
moist, yet you feel that its belly encases a great secret, as though
it were a woman of boundless passion preparing to meet her
mate. The earth is motionless, but its bowels are astir with
gushing water, the water of life and fertility. The earth is moist
and ready; it prepares itself for giving. Something sharp pierces
the bowels of the earth; there is a moment of ecstasy, of pain, of
giving, and in the place where the bowels of the earth have been
pierced the seed flows in, just as the female womb embraces the
embryo in tenderness, warmth, and love. So the innermost part of
the earth encases the seed of wheat, maize and bean, and tomorrow the earth will split open and send forth vegatation and fruit.

Ni'ma remembered that, as a child, when the women used to
come on visits to her mother, they would seat her on their laps
and stroke her luxuriant hair which hung down on to her
shoulders, would kiss her on the cheek and lips, and would
tickle her and hug her to their bosoms. She used to hate it and
would squirm about in their arms. Once she was enraged by
the way in which a fat woman was fussing over her; feeling the
woman's thick arms encircling her like the jaws of some wild
animal, her heavy haunches and pungent perfume, it was as
though she were being throttled. She fidgeted and tried to
escape from the woman's grasp but the woman hugged her
closely to her breast, swooping down on her face with pinched
lips, kissing her on neck and cheek, and puffing at her. Ni'ma
then gave her a hearty slap on the face at which, in alarm,

the woman let go and Ni'ma made her escape from the room. When she grew up and was no longer a child, the heads of both men and women would turn as she passed them on the road; yet her beauty meant nothing to her. She also recollected how she had forced her father to put her into the elementary school to learn the Koran, where she had been a lone girl amongst boys. After one month she had learnt how to write, for she used to listen to boys older than herself reading aloud chapters from the Koran and these stuck in her mind. She applied herself to the Koran, eagerly committing it to memory and finding joy in reciting it. Certain verses gave her particular pleasure and they would strike upon her heart like good news. Of the bits she had learnt by heart she liked best the *Chapter of the Merciful*, the *Chapter of Mary*, and the *Chapter of Retribution*, and would feel her heart being wrung with sadness as she read about Job. When she reached the verse 'And we restored unto him his family, and as many more with them, through our mercy', she would picture 'Mercy' to herself as a woman, a woman of rare beauty, dedicated to the service of her husband, and she wished that her parents had named her Rahma, that is 'Mercy'. She used to dream that one day she would make some great sacrifice, though she did not know what form it would take, and then she would experience the same strange sensation that came over her when reading the *Chapter of Mary*.

Ni'ma grew up a serious child, the pivot of her personality being a sense of responsibility. She would share the household chores with her mother and would talk everything over with her; with her father she would have frank, grown-up discussions that would sometimes astonish him.

Her brother, who was two years older, used to urge her to continue her education at school and would say to her: 'You could become a doctor or a lawyer', but she did not believe in that type of education.

With that impenetrable mask of gravity on her face, she would say to her brother, 'Education at school is a whole lot of nonsense. It's quite enough to read and write and to know the Koran and the rituals of prayer'.

Her brother would laugh and say, 'Tomorrow some nice lad will come along and marry you and spare us all this bother!'

The members of her family would say such things to her with a feeling of trepidation, for they realised that this girl with the grave countenance and the sullen eyes held something within her heart that she concealed from them. When she was sixteen, her mother began talking about the young men who would make suitable husbands: the rich, the educated, the handsome, and those whose mothers and fathers would be suitable as 'in-laws'. But Ni'ma would shrug her shoulders and say nothing. And when Amna had come to talk to Saadiyya about Ni'ma marrying Ahmed and Saadiyya had said to her, 'The decision lies with the girl's father', she had known in her heart of hearts that it lay with no one but Ni'ma herself. She had had to be informed, at which she had shrugged her shoulders and said, 'I'm not ready to marry yet,' and it was senseless to argue with her—especially as Saadiyya was not keen on becoming related to Amna's family.

Not long after that another suitor made his appearance: Idris. Many a girl in the village would have been only too happy to be his wife, for he was an educated man, worked as a teacher at an Intermediate School, was of a gentle disposition and well-respected locally. Though he was not from one of the well-connected and prominent families in the village, his father had nevertheless made a place for himself through his diligence and good neighbourliness. It was a good, comfortably off family. Hajj Ibrahim, Ni'ma's father, her mother Saadiyya, and her three brothers, were for accepting Idris. Ni'ma, however, was of another opinion. 'He's not for me,' she said with a shrug of her shoulders. Hajj Ibrahim spoke furiously to her and was about to slap her. Suddenly, though, he stopped; something in the girl's stubborn countenance killed the anger in his breast. Perhaps it was the expression of her eyes, perhaps the calm resolution on her face. It was as though the man sensed that this girl was neither disobedient nor refractory, but that she was propelled by an inner counsel to embark upon something from which no one could deflect her. From that day on no one talked to her about marriage.

When Ni'ma was alone with her thoughts and the idea of marriage crossed her mind, she had the feeling that marriage would come to her unexpectedly and unplanned, just as God's divine decree falls upon His servants—as people are born, fall ill, and die. As the Nile floods its banks, storms rage, the date palms produce their fruit each year, as the corn sprouts, the rain pours down, and the seasons change, so would her marriage be: a destiny fore-ordained by God for her from before she was born, before the Nile began to flow, before God created the earth and all that is on it. She felt no joy, fear or distress when she thought of it, merely that a great responsibility would be placed upon her shoulders at some time, be it near at hand or far off. Each girl-friend of hers in the district grew up with a specific image of the knight who would tether his steed outside the house one bright evening and come in and snatch her off from amidst her family, fleeing with her far away to magical worlds of happiness and plenty. But for Ni'ma no such set image had been formed in her mind. As she grew up, so there grew up with her the idea of an overwhelming love which she would one day bestow upon some man. The man might well be already married with children and would take her as his second wife; he might be a handsome and educated young man; or yet a farmer from among the ordinary folk of the village, with legs and feet cracked from having spent so much time wading about in water and wielding a hoe. He could, again, be Zein, and when Zein came to Ni'ma's mind, she experienced a sensation of warmth in her heart, of the kind a mother feels for her children. Intermingled with it was another feeling: of pity. She would see Zein as being an orphan in need of being cared for. In any case he was her cousin, and there was nothing unusual in the fact that she should feel concern for him.

Zein's mother did not worry as to where he spent the night, for, like a restless soul, he had no fixed abode. Whenever, though, a wedding party was being held, you'd be sure to find Zein there: among the Talha people or with the Koz bedouin, be it up river or down; neither cold nor raging storm at night, not even the swollen Nile at the time of its flooding, would keep him away. With rare sensitivity his ear would detect women's ululations from miles away, at which he would throw his robe over his shoulder and hurry off as though drawn to the source of the sound. Sometimes a light would flash suddenly from behind the sand dunes as the lorries made their way from Omdurman and would show up a thin figure trudging along through the sands, his body leaning slightly forward, his eyes looking down at the ground, as he hastened eastwards. Recognising Zein, the passengers would know that some wedding party was being held on the outskirts of the village and they would either call out at him as they passed or would stop the lorry and banter with him. Sometimes there would be a whole crowd of people walking behind him.

The trilling sounds of joy from the women would draw nearer, become more clear cut, till Zein was able to distinguish the voices of the various women. Then the lights came into view, also the assembled shapes that rose and fell like devils in the Valley of the Jinn. Then could be seen the dust that was raised by the feet of people dancing, caught in the strands of light. All of a sudden the night would be shattered by a call that everyone knew: 'Hear ye, people of the wedding, men of the dance, Zein has come to you.' And with a leap Zein would land like Destiny herself in the dance circle. Suddenly the place would quicken into life, for Zein would have imbued it with new vigour. From afar one could hear their shouts as they greeted him: 'Welcome! Welcome! Join in the company!' When the women's voices died in their throats and the lights went out and the people went off to their homes, Zein would rest his head against a stone or the trunk of a tree and would, as birds do, take a quick nap. When the muezzin gave the call to dawn prayers, he would take himself back to his people and wake up his mother for her to make tea.

One morning, though, the muezzin gave his call and Zein did not return. The eastern horizon grew red just before sunrise, then the sun rose up to the height of a man and still Zein had not returned. Zein's mother, experiencing a slight quivering sensation in her left side, had ominous forebodings, for she held the opinion that if there was a quivering in her left side harm would surely befall someone in her family, and she thought of going to Zein's uncle. Then she heard a movement at the courtyard door, heard the large door creak, then a loud crash, and found herself all of a sudden face to face with a terrible sight. She gave a scream which was heard by Hajj Ibrahim, Ni'ma's father, four houses away where he was sitting on his prayer-mat drinking his early morning cup of coffee. The house filled with people, men and women, and they bore Zein's mother off unconscious. The people split up into two groups, one going off with the mother, and the other, mostly composed of men, gathering round Zein, whose head bore a large wound stretching right up to near his right eye, while his chest, outer robe and trousers were stained with blood. The people lost their heads and Abdul Hafeez began shouting at Zein, his eyes reddened with anger: 'Tell us who did this to you—who's the criminal dog who struck you?' The women screamed and some of them began weeping. Ni'ma stood looking on from afar, silent, her eyes fixed on Zein's face, the sullenness in them having been replaced by a great tenderness. 'The doctor!' said Hajj Ibrahim, and the words fell like water on fire. The women's wailing died down. Mahjoub called out, 'The doctor!' Then Abdul Hafeez called out, 'The doctor!' and Ahmed Isma'il set off on his donkey to fetch him.

When Zein returned from the hospital in Merowi after a stay of two weeks, his face was sparkling clean and his clothes a spotless white. When he laughed, people no longer saw those two yellow fangs in his mouth, but a row of gleaming white teeth in his upper jaw and another row of pearly dentures in his lower. It was as though Zein had been transformed into another person—and it struck Ni'ma, as she stood among the ranks of people come out to meet him, that Zein was not in fact devoid of a certain handsomeness.

For a long time after that Zein could talk of nothing else but his trip to Merowi. He enjoyed it when his old friends— Mahjoub, Abdul Hafeez, Ahmed Isma'il, Hamad Wad Rayyis, Taher Rawwasi and Sa'eed the merchant—gathered round him and he would relate to them what had happened.

'Directly I arrived they took my clothes off and dressed me in clean ones. The bed was a splendid affair, the sheets as white as milk, and the stone floors so highly polished you slid around on the rugs'.

'Never mind about the rugs and stone floors,' Mahjoub interrupted him banteringly. 'What did they fill that great stomach of yours with?'

Zein's mouth trembled as though he were about to tuck in to a banquet. 'Now you're talking! Merowi Hospital's food— there's nothing like it. There wasn't any sort of food they didn't have—fish dishes, egg dishes, dishes of roast meat, dishes of chicken.'

'But aren't the helpings in the hospital a bit small?' Mahjoub again interrupted him. 'How did you manage to get enough?'

Zein gave a wide, knowing smile, revealing his new teeth. 'Because my nurse took a fancy to me'.

'There is no god but God,' exclaimed Abdul Hafeez. 'You good-for-nothing, were you even flirting with the nurses?'

Zein's body shook with stifled laughter. 'Oh yes, believe me she was quite a wench.'

Hamad Wad Rayyis, who up to now had been listening and laughing but not saying anything, intervened with: 'The Prophet bless you, Zein—give us a description of her.'

Zein looked behind him as though frightened that someone might overhear him and lowered his voice: 'God save us, men, she had quite a backside on her!'

The thread of the conversation was broken for a time as the assembly rocked with laughter. When Hamad Wad Rayyis had recovered his breath—though vestiges of laughter still remained in his chest—he said: 'What did you do to her, you rascal?'

'The wench was from Omdurman,' Zein continued as though not having heard the last question. 'She was smooth-cheeked without cuts.'

Wad Rayyis crawled up close to Zein and repeated his question in another form: 'And how did you come to know she had a large backside?'

Zein immediately retorted: 'Did they tell you I'm blind? Can't I see what's there right in front of me?'

Mahjoub, delighted at the reply and looking at Wad Rayyis, said: 'The scoundrel knows what's what.'

Zein put his hands behind his head, and leaned backwards slightly; then, with a mischievous smile on his face, he slowly said: 'Do you want to know, men, what I did to her?'

Eagerly Wad Rayyis said, 'By the Prophet, Zein, tell us what you did to her.'

Zein's smile widened, then he opened his mouth to speak and some of the light from the large lamp hanging in Sa'eed's shop was reflected on his teeth. But suddenly, at a bound, he was on his feet, just as though he'd been stung by a scorpion. Up jumped Ahmed Isma'il and Mahjoub, Taher Rawwasi and Hamad Wad Rayyis. 'Hold on to him,' shouted Abdul Hafeez. Zein, though, was quicker than them and in a flash had seized hold of his man, had raised him high in the air and thrown him to the ground. Then he tightened his grip on his throat. They all fell upon Zein, Ahmed Isma'il seizing hold of his right arm, Abdul Hafeez of his left, with Taher Rawwasi taking him by the middle, and Hamad Wad Rayyis by his legs. Sa'eed, who was weighing out something in his shop, hurried out and also took hold of Zein's legs. Even so they were not successful.

There flowed into Zein's lean body an immensely terrifying strength with which no one could deal. All the inhabitants of the village knew of this fearful strength and stood in awe of it, and Zein's family did all they could to see he did not use it against anyone. They would shake in terror when they remembered how Zein had once seized a difficult calf by the horns, had lifted it from the ground like a bundle of hay, and had then swung it round and thrown it to the ground; how, too, in one of his fits of excitement, he had torn an acacia bush up by the roots as though it were a stick of maize. They all knew that this emaciated body concealed an extraordinary, super-human strength and that Seif ad-Din—the prey upon whom Zein swooped—was doomed. For a while their various voices were intertwined. 'The he-donkey, I'll kill him,' Zein was repeating angrily. Abdul Hafeez's voice was raised, tense and afraid: 'By the Prophet, Zein—for God's sake, let him be.' Mahjoub began swearing in desperation. Ahmed Isma'il, the youngest and strongest of them, at a loss as to what to do next, bit Zein in the back. Taher Rawwasi, too, was a man famed for his strength and could swim the Nile back and forth, staying under the water for minutes on end, in his search for fish at night. His strength, though, was nothing in comparison with Zein's. Amidst their clamour they heard a snorting sound emanating from Seif ad-Din's throat and saw him striking out at the air with his long legs. 'He's dead, he's killed him,' shouted Mahjoub.

But suddenly a new voice, that of Haneen, rose calm and serene above the hubbub: 'Zein the blessed, may God be pleased with you.' Zein released his grip and Seif ad-Din fell limply to the ground. The six men also dropped down in a heap, for Haneen's voice had surprised them and they had been taken unawares by Zein's sudden immobility—it was as though there had been a wall in front of them that had suddenly collapsed. A very short instant passed, something of the order of the twinkling of an eye, during which complete silence reigned, a silence that was inevitably a mixture of terror, consternation, and hope. After that, life once again welled up within them and they remembered Seif ad-Din. Their heads bent over him, and then Mahjoub called out in a joyful, trembling voice: 'Thanks be to God. Thanks be to God.' They carried Seif ad-Din off and put him on a bench in front of Sa'eed's shop, and with voices tense and low, they began bringing him back to life. Only then did they remember Zein and notice him sitting on his backside, his hands between his knees, with his head bowed. Haneen had placed his hand with extreme tenderness on Zein's shoulder and was talking to him in a voice firm but filled with love. 'Zein, blessed one of God, why did you do it?'

Mahjoub came up and scolded Zein, but Haneen silenced him with a look. 'If you hadn't come, reverend Sheikh, he'd have killed him,' Mahjoub said to Haneen after a while. Ahmed Isma'il and Taher Rawwasi joined them, while Abdul Hafeez, Sa'eed the merchant, and Wad Rayyis stayed with Seif ad-Din.

After a time, his head still bowed, Zein repeated what Mahjoub had said: 'If you hadn't come, reverend Sheikh, I'd have killed him. The he-donkey—when he struck me on the head with an axe did he think I'd let him get away with it.' There was no anger in his voice, the tone being more like that of his natural gaiety; though the others remained silent, they too were infected by this feeling of lightheartedness.

'But you were in the wrong,' said Haneen.

Zein remained silent. 'When did Seif ad-Din strike you on the head with an axe?' continued Haneen.

'At the time of his sister's wedding,' replied Zein laughing, his face full of mirth.

'What did you do to his sister on her wedding day?'

'His sister had her eye on me. Why did they want to marry her off to that good-for-nothing fellow?'

Ahmed Isma'il could not help laughing.

'All the girls are after you, blessed one of God,' Haneen said in a more gentle and tender voice. 'Tomorrow you'll be marrying the best girl in the village.'

Mahjoub felt a slight palpitation of his heart; having an innate awe of religious people, specially ascetics like Haneen, he used to remove himself from their path and have nothing to do with them. Yet he took warning of their predictions, feeling, despite his lack of outward concern, that they had mysterious powers. 'The predictions of such ascetics are not made fruitlessly,' he would say to himself. It was perhaps this that made him say in a loud voice tinged with contempt: 'Who would marry this imbecile? On top of everything he was going to commit a crime.'

Haneen gave Mahjoub a stern look, and though Mahjoub trembled inwardly, he did not show his fear. 'Zein's no imbecile,' said Haneen. 'Zein's a blessed person. Tomorrow he'll be marrying the best girl in the village.'

Suddenly Zein gave an insolent, childish laugh and said: 'I wanted to kill him, the he-donkey of a man—splitting me open with an axe just because his sister had her eye on me.'

'Now we want you to make it up,' said Haneen firmly. 'Let it end there—it's over and done with. He hit you and now you've hit him.' He called Seif ad-Din, whose tall form approached, surrounded by Sa'eed, Abdul Hafeez and Hamad Wad Rayyis. 'Get up and kiss him on the head,' Haneen said to Zein, and without protest Zein got up, took hold of Seif ad-Din's head and kissed him. Then he bent over Haneen's head and covered it with kisses, saying, 'Our Sheikh Haneen. Our father, blessed of God.' It was a stirring moment that silenced them all.

Seif ad-Din's eyes were wet with tears. 'I have wronged you,' he said to Zein. 'Forgive me.' He got up and kissed Zein's head, then seized Haneen's hand and kissed it. All the men came along: Mahjoub, Abdul Hafeez, Hamad Wad Rayyis, Taher Rawwasi, Ahmed Isma'il, and Sa'eed the merchant. Each silently took hold of Haneen's hand and kissed it.

'God bless you. God bring down His blessings upon you,' said Haneen in his soft, unassuming voice, and he rose and took up his pitcher.

'You must dine with us tonight,' Mahjoub quickly invited him.

Haneen, though, gently refused. Clasping Zein's shoulder with the other hand, he said, 'Dinner's to be in the house of the blessed one,' and the two of them made off into the darkness. For an instant a shaft of light from the lamp hanging in Sa'eed's shop flickered above their heads, then slipped off them as a white silk gown slips from a man's shoulder. Mahjoub looked at Abdul Hafeez, Sa'eed looked at Seif ad-Din, and they all exchanged looks and nodded their heads.

Long years after this incident, when Mahjoub had become a grandfather many times over, as had Abdul Hafeez, Taher Rawwasi and the rest, when Ahmed Isma'il had become a father and his daughters had become of marriageable age, the inhabitants of the village used to look back on that year and

on the incident with Zein, Haneen, and Seif ad-Din that had
taken place in front of Sa'eed's shop. Those who had taken
part in the incident remember it with solemn awe—including
Mahjoub who had never previously bothered about anything.
The lives of each one of those eight men, the participants
in the incident, were affected in one way or another. In the
days that were ahead of them these eight men were to go over
the details of the incident among themselves thousands of
times, and each time the events made a more magical impression.
They would remember in amazement how Haneen had
appeared to them from out of the blue at the moment, the very
instant, when Zein's grip had tightened on Seif ad-Din and
he had all but throttled him. In fact some of them insist that
Seif ad-Din had actually died, had breathed his last, and
had fallen to the ground a lifeless corpse. Seif ad-Din himself
affirms this version and says that he did actually die; he says
that the moment Zein's grip on his throat had tightened he
completely departed this world. He saw a vast crocodile
the size of a large ox with its mouth agape; the crocodile's
jaws closed upon him, then came a wave so large it seemed
like a mountain, which bore off the crocodile with Seif ad-Din
between its jaws into the valley that was the trough of the
wave, and the crocodile plunged down into a vast bottomless
pit. It was then, Seif ad-Din says, that he saw Death face to
face, and Abdul Hafeez, the person closest to Seif ad-Din when
he recovered consciousness, is adamant that the first words
he uttered on breath coming anew to his lungs, the first thing
he said on opening his eyes, was: 'I bear witness that there
is no god but God, and I bear witness that Mohammed is

the Messenger of God.' At any event, there is no doubt that from that moment Seif ad-Din's life underwent a change undreamt of by anyone.

Seif ad-Din was the only son of Badawi the Jeweller— so named because he had followed this trade at the beginning of his life, and when he had grown rich and was no longer a jeweller, the name had inevitably stuck to him. Badawi was well-off, possibly the richest man in the village. Some of his wealth he had collected by the sweat of his brow from his trade as a goldsmith, from commerce and travelling about; some had come to him from his wife. He was, as the village folk expressed it, a man 'with a green arm,' who touched nothing without it turning to money. In less than twenty years he had built up a fortune from scratch, partly in lands and estates, partly in goods distributed along the length of the Nile from Kareema to Karma, partly in the form of boats loaded with dates and merchandise plying up and down the river; partly in the shape of the great mass of gold worn by his wife and daughters in the way of jewellery covering their necks and arms. Seif ad-Din was brought up an only son among five daughters, pampered by his mother, pampered by his father, and pampered by his five sisters. He could not but be spoilt, or, as the village folk put it, he could not but become soft and flabby like the tree that grows in the shade of a bigger tree, being exposed to no winds and not seeing the light of the sun.

Badawi died with a bitter lump of disappointment in his throat because of his son. He had spent a lot of money on his education, but the boy had done no good. He had set him

up in the village in a business, which had failed within a month.
After this he had put him into a workshop to learn a trade,
but he had run away. In the end, by bringing influence to bear,
he had succeeded in having him appointed as a junior government employee, hoping that he would learn to stand on his own
feet. But no more than a few months later a succession of
reports came, both from the mouths of enemies and friends,
from those who enjoyed such misfortunes and those who were
well-wishers, that his son was spending all his nights in a
wine-shop and was seen at office only once or twice a week,
and that his superiors had warned him time and time again,
threatening him with dismissal. The father had therefore set
off for the city, to return herding along his son like a captive,
having sworn he would keep him imprisoned in the fields his
whole life long, like a man in bondage. Those were his words.

And so Seif ad-Din had spent a year collecting fodder for
the cows, pasturing the cattle on the fringes of the fields all
day long, sowing and harvesting, chopping wood and grumb-
ling. Even so, he did not lack amusement of an evening, for he
knew of places where liquor was made and would frequent the
girls who used to make it—'the sluts' as the villagers called
them. These girls were slaves who had been given their
freedom, some of them having migrated from the village and
married far away from the locality of their bondage; others
had married freed slaves in the village and led a respectable
life, a continuing affection existing between them and their
former masters. Some of them, however, not finding a settled
life easy, had stayed on the perimeter of life in the village,
a place of call for those bent on pleasure and sensual enjoy-

ment. The fact was that this rendezvous of ex-slave-girls was something alien that contained the spirit of adventure and rebellion; it represented a departure from the familiar. There, on the edge of the desert far from the village, squatted their houses made of straw, and at night, when people had gone to bed, beams of lamp-light flickered from their doorways and windows, and drunken laughter could be heard. In their displeasure the inhabitants of the village burned them down, but they returned to life like the alfa plant that will not die. Though the villagers drove away those who inhabited these houses, tormenting them in a variety of ways, they soon got together again, like flies alighting upon a dead cow. How many an adolescent young man's heart had throbbed in the darkness as the night brought him the sounds of female laughter and the shouts of intoxicated men. In that 'oasis' on the edge of the desert there was something frightening, something delightful yet intimidating that tempted one to reconnoitre.

It was not difficult for Seif ad-Din to find his way to it. There he would spend his nights, for he had taken one of the women as his mistress. All this his father bore patiently. When reports came to him about his son, he would sometimes pretend to take no notice, at others he would fly into a rage. But his patience came to an end when, one night as he sat on his prayer-mat after performing the evening prayer, Seif ad-Din came to him reeking of liquor. In a voice made hoarse from the effects of drink and lack of sleep Seif ad-Din announced that he was in love with and wanted to marry Sarra, one of the ex-slave-girls. The father saw red and lost all control: his only son, a dissolute drunkard, informing him, as he sat on his prayer-mat, that he was 'in love'—a phrase that conjured up in the minds of fathers in the village all the concepts of idleness, indolence, and lack of manliness; and that he wanted to marry some brazen, immoral slave-girl. The father rose and set about giving his son a thorough good beating. Along came the mother wailing loudly, at which people gathered and finally extricated the son from the father's hands more dead than alive. The father swore that the dissolute boy—as he expressed it—was not to spend another single night under his roof, and that he disowned him as a son. Seif ad-Din spent the night at his uncle's house, vanishing the next morning.

Jeweller Badawi passed the rest of his life like a man stricken with some infirmity. Pain bit into his heart and his face became as thin and emaciated as a consumptive's. He used to say that his son had died; when sometimes, by a slip of the tongue, he mentioned his son he did so as though he had in actual fact died. Dreadful reports about Seif ad-Din were continually being received: of how he had been sent to prison in Khartoum on a charge of larceny; of how he had once been accused in Port Sudan of killing a man and would have been hanged had the real murderer not eventually been found; and of how he lived like an out-and-out dissolute wastrel with the prostitutes of every town in which he stayed. Once he was reported to be working as a labourer carrying bales of cotton on his back in the port; another time that he was a lorry driver between Fasher and Obeid; on yet other occasions he was said to be cultivating cotton at Toker.

His uncles on both sides of the family tried to persuade his father to write a will leaving all his fortune to his wife and daughters. All sensible men in the village also held that this was the right thing to do, but the father continually shirked it, explaining that he would do so when he felt his end drawing near and that he was still in good health and was in no need of writing a will. These men used to shake their heads in distress and say that Badawi was still hoping his son would return to his senses; something incomprehensible to the inhabitants of the village stopped the man from taking the decisive step of cutting his son off from his inheritance.

Then, one night in the month of Ramadan, Badawi died seated on his prayer-mat after having performed the special late night prayers for this month. He was a good man, and he died the death of all good men, in the month of Ramadan, in the final third of it—the most blessed part—on his prayer-mat after having performed the special Ramadan prayers. The people of the village shook their heads and said: 'God have mercy on Badawi. He was a good man. He deserved a better son than that dissolute one of his.'

One day when the people were still in mourning and had just finished giving the prescribed alms, Seif ad-Din made his appearance. He carried a thick stick of the sort used in the east of the Sudan and had no luggage whatsoever. His hair was ruffled as a *sayal* acacia tree, his beard thick and dirty, and his face that of a man who has come back from Hell-fire. He gave greeting to no one and all eyes avoided him. However, his eldest uncle on his father's side walked up to him and spat in his face, and when the news of his arrival reached his mother in the other side of the house where she was leading the women of the household in their mourning of the deceased, she broke into renewed wailing as though her husband had just died. Seif ad-Din's sisters broke into wailing, as did all his aunts, and the women's wing of the house fairly rocked with the din, until the eldest uncle went and rebuked them, at which they fell silent.

All this did not prevent Seif ad-Din from getting his hands on his father's wealth. All the uncles managed to do was to rescue his mother's and sisters' portions, leaving the greater part of the fortune in Seif ad-Din's hands. Here, too, began the life of torture for Mousa, Zein's friend—Mousa the Lame as the village folk called him. Saif ad-Din turned him out on the pretext that as he was no longer a slave he was not responsible for him. From then on Seif ad-Din led an unrestrained life, made worse by the abundance of money he now possessed. He was continually away travelling, sometimes eastwards, sometimes westwards, spending a month in Khartoum, a month in Cairo, a month in Asmara, only coming to the village to sell some land or dispose of a crop. He was a type of person the inhabitants of the village had never in their lives known and they shunned him as they would a leper; even those closest to him on both sides of his family did not feel safe having him in their homes and would shut the door in his face lest he corrupt their sons or seduce their daughters.

On one of his intermittent visits to the village he found his sister's marriage in progress—his family kept him away from their weddings and he by natural disposition did not attend funerals. Because of him that marriage was all but transformed into a tragedy. First of all, there was the incident of Zein. Along came Zein as usual with his gaiety and raillery, with no one paying him any heed. Seif ad-Din, however, taking exception to this, struck him on the head with an axe. The matter would have ended in prison had it not been for the intervention of the wise men of the village who said that Seif ad-Din was not worth the time they would spend on him in the courts. Secondly, the bridegroom almost changed his mind at the last moment because he quarrelled with Seif ad-Din, the bride's brother, and once again the wise men of the village, amongst them the bridegroom's father, gathered together and said that Seif ad-Din was not one of them and that his attendance at the weddng was an unavoidable evil. Thirdly, in the last week of the marriage celebrations, tens of strangers whom no one had ever seen before descended upon the house: brazen women, and men with lascivious glances, vagabonds and insolent boors, who came from who knows where—friends of Seif ad-Din's, invited by him to his sister's wedding celebrations. At this point the inhabitants of the village found themselves bound to do something; thus, before these guests had settled in their seats, there entered a file of men from the village headed by Ahmed Isma'il and then Mahjoub, followed by Abdul Hafeez, Taher Rawwasi and Hamad Wad Rayyes,then all Seif ad-Din's uncles—about thirty men with stout sticks and hoes in their hands. Locking the doors behind them, they gave a good beating to all the intruders and the best hiding of all they gave to Seif ad-Din. Then they threw them out into the street.

While the whole village was in a turmoil from that affliction called Seif ad-Din, all of a sudden, following the Haneen incident, he changed as though born anew. To begin with people couldn't believe their eyes, but every day Seif ad-Din did something new. First they heard that he had gone early one morning to his mother, had kissed her head and wept lengthily before her. Hardly had they got over this than they heard he had brought together all his uncles, and had repented and asked forgiveness in front of them, and that as an assurance of his repentance he had taken all that remained of his father's fortune from his own charge and had made his senior paternal uncle a trustee over it, until he should become wholly fit for carrying out his responsibilities. No sooner had the inhabitants of the village accustomed their ears to that than to their amazement they saw Seif ad-Din repairing to the mosque for the Friday prayers. He had shaved off his beard, and had his moustache neatly trimmed, and was dressed in clean clothes. Those who attended the prayers said that when he heard the Imam's sermon, the subject of which was the honouring of one's parents, he burst into such lengthy weeping that he went into a swoon and the people flocked round to comfort him. On leaving the mosque he had immediately gone to Mousa the Lame and, telling him that he had acted wrongly towards him, had asked his forgiveness and informed him that he would treat him as his father used to do. For a month or so the village never stopped gasping as every day it heard of some new act performed by Seif ad-Din: his abstaining from wine, his withdrawal from the company of his disreputable friends, his devoting himself to his prayers, his applying himself to reviving his father's business which he had under-mined, his engagement to his cousin, and finally his resolution to perform the pilgrimage that year. Whenever Abdul Hafeez, who was one of those who believed most firmly in Haneen's

miracles as evidenced in Seif ad-Din, heard some fresh piece
of news, he would hurry off to Mahjoub, who was known for
his distaste for religious people and in particular ascetics. 'A
miracle, my friend—not a doubt about it.' Mahjoub would
keep silent—in his belly a sensation of vague uneasiness assails
him in such circumstances. 'Seif ad-Din has decided to go on
the pilgrimage. By God, do you credit it, friend? Do you or
don't you believe it? A miracle, friend, without the shadow of
a doubt.' At first Mahjoub used to say to Abdul Hafeez that
Seif ad-Din had had enough of fooling about or, as he put
it, 'His fooling about had reached the giddy limit,' and that he
was bound to make a change one day. But as he went on
hearing something new and astounding each day, he no
longer felt capable of disputing the matter and took refuge
in silence.

The miraculous change in Seif ad-Din saw the beginning of
a number of strange things that came to pass in the village
that year. There was not the slightest doubt in anyone's mind,
even Mahjoub's, as they saw miracle after miracle occurring,
that it was all attributable to Haneen's having said to those
eight men in front of Sa'eed's shop that night, 'God bless you
all. May God bring you His blessing.' The time was a little
before the evening prayer, a time especially propitious for
prayers—especially when made by such saints of God as
Haneen. The village was still and silent, except for a slight
fresh breeze that played with the fronds of the palm trees.
The eight men who were witnesses, and the rest of the people
in their houses and fields, they all remember that night as

clearly as though it were yesterday. The thick velvety darkness lay over every corner of the village, except for the faint beams of light leaking out from the windows of the houses and the bright light from the large lamp in Sa'eed's shop. The time was that of the seasonal changeover from summer to autumn. Sa'eed the shopkeeper remembers that the night had not been scorchingly hot like its predecessor and that his face was not moist with sweat as he weighed out sugar for Seif ad-Din, and that when 'the hullabaloo occurred,' as he put it, and he left his scales and went out of his shop to intervene between Zein and Seif ad-Din, he remembers a cold breeze blowing on his face. The people who did not have the good fortune to be present at the incident, because they were preparing for evening prayers in the mosque, mention that as he led them in prayer that night the Imam recited a section of the *Chapter of Mary*. Hajj Ibrahim, Zein's uncle and Ni'ma's father, a man renowned for his truthfulness, states quite definitely that the Imam read the verse: 'And shake towards thee the trunk of the palm tree, it will drop upon thee fresh dates fit to gather' from the *Chapter of Mary*, a verse which is a particularly auspicious and blessed one. Hamad Wad Rayyis, who is well-known in the village for the range of his imagination and a propensity for exaggeration, adds that on the night in question a comet appeared on the western horizon over the burial grounds. However, no one except him mentions a comet. In any event there is no doubt about Haneen, that righteous man, saying within the hearing of eight men on that auspicious night between summer and autumn, just a little before the evening prayer, 'God bless you all. May God bring you His blessing,' and it was as though supernatural powers in the heavens had answered in one voice 'Amen'.

After that, supernatural events came in quick succession, miracle following miracle in a fascinating manner. During its existence the village had never experienced such an auspicious and fruitful year as 'Haneen's year,' as they had begun to call it. It was certainly true that the prices of cotton had had an unprecedented rise that year and that the government, for the first time in history, had permitted them to cultivate it, whereas previously it had been restricted to specified districts of the country. (Mahjoub alone, and on his own admission, made more than a thousand pounds from his cotton.) It is true, too, that for no particular reason—or for some obscure one they didn't know about—a large army camp was set up in the desert two miles from the village. Soldiers eat and drink, and so the village benefitted from supplying vegetables, meat, fruit, and milk to the army. Even the prices of dates had an unprecedented rise that year. Also true is the fact that the government, that creature which in their anecdotes they likened to a refractory donkey, decided all at once—again for no apparent reason—to build in their village, to the exclusion of the rest of the villages of the northern sector of the country, a large hospital for five hundred patients, a secondary school, and an agricultural school—all this despite the fact that they were people without power or influence and with no spokesman to talk on their behalf in the assemblies of the powers-that-be. Here again the village benefitted through supplying the labour, the building materials, and the food, to

say nothing of the fact that the sick among them were assured
of treatment and that their sons would obtain proper education.
If all these indications do not suffice, how do you explain that
the government, that 'refractory donkey' as they believed,
also decided that very same year, no more than two months
having passed on Haneen's death, to organise their lands into
a large agricultural project which the government itself, with
all its power and authority, would supervise? Suddenly they
found their village alive with land surveyors, engineers, and
inspectors. When the government has made up its mind to
something, it has the power to carry it out, and it was merely
a question of day following upon day and month succeeding
month before there rose up on the bank of the Nile by their
village a lofty, temple-like building of red brick which cast
its shadow upon the river. A little later, amidst the din of
labourers and the grating of iron, the wheels of the giant
began to turn and its pumps began sucking up such quantities
of waters from the Nile as ten water-wheels during tens of days
would not have managed—all in a flash, like a man sucking up
his tea. And so the vast tract of land from the bank of the Nile
to the edge of the desert was inundated with water. Some of it
was land that had not seen water from early times, and there it
was, after a while, swelling with life. How could this be
explained? Abdul Hafeez, though, knows the secret. Scanning
the expanse of field which is his, as the wind plays with the
wheat so that its ranks bend down like graceful houris drying
their hair in the breeze, he says to Mahjoub, 'A miracle, my
friend—without the slightest doubt.'

Tureifi sat down furtively in his chair after having told

the Headmaster of the news of Zein's marriage. He seated himself on the edge of his behind as though preparing himself for flight at any instant—there was something of the hyena about both his manner and his nature. Looking around him with cunning eyes, he whispered in the ear of his right-hand neighbour, 'We've got out of tonight's geography. I bet you the Headmaster won't finish the lesson.'

As predicted by Tureifi, the Headmaster announced in a listless, offhand voice that he was going out on an urgent matter. 'Revise the lesson on the wheat-growing area of Canada,' and he went out with constrained steps as, watched by Tureifi, he attempted not to hurry until he got to the door of the school courtyard. Tureifi gave a mischievous laugh when he saw the Headmaster grasp the end of his *aba* and rush forward through the sand as hard as he could go.

The Headmaster reached Sheikh Ali's shop in the market, panting for breath and dry of throat, the school not being all that near to the market and the two being separated by a tract of sand into which one's feet sank; besides, the headmaster was in his fifties. Sheikh Ali's shop in the market was his favourite haunt. He was also delighted to see Abdul Samad with whom he had a bitter-sweet relationship and without whose presence he could never really enjoy any gathering or game of back-gammon. Though still ten yards away from the shop, he couldn't help starting to speak: 'Sheikh Ali, Hajj Abdul Samad— this year's a year of miracles. What a thing to happen!'

The last sentence brought him to them and they sat him down in his favourite seat—a low wood and cord armchair.

The coffee was still hot and gave off an aroma of canella

bark, cardamom, and ginger. Taking hold of the cup he brought it to his mouth, then quickly replaced it. 'Is the news true?' he said.

'Drink up your coffee before it gets cold,' Abdul Samad said with a laugh to the Headmaster. 'What they say is quite right.'

Shifting the quid of tobacco from the right side of his mouth to the left, Sheikh Ali said, 'The story of Zein's marriage? It's a hundred per cent true all right.'

The Headmaster took a large gulp from his cup of coffee, placed it on the small table in front of him, and lit himself a cigarette and took a deep pull.

'My dear fellow, this is a most strange year—or am I wrong?' The Headmaster did not use the expression 'chap' or 'man' like the other villagers, but would begin his sentences by using the phrase 'my dear fellow.'

'What you say is quite right, Headmaster,' said Abdul Samad. 'A really extraordinary year. Women who'd given up hope of ever being pregnant suddenly have children; cows and sheep give birth to two or three—.' Hajj Ali continued to enumerate the miracles that had taken place that year: 'The dates from the palm trees were so plentiful we couldn't find enough sacks to carry them in; also it snowed—can you imagine such a thing? Snow falling from the sky on a desert town like this?' The Headmaster shook his head and Abdul Samad muttered incoherent words, for the fall of snow that year had been something to amaze them all, and the Headmaster, for all his vast knowledge of geography, could find no explanation for it.

'But the biggest miracle of all,' said the Headmaster, 'is the business of Zein's betrothal.' (He had the habit of interspersing his speech with words in the classical language)

'One is loath to believe it,' said Sheikh Ali—who was, like Abdul Samad, infected by the Headmaster's classical words; and they would both try to vie with him.

'Haneen's words were not idle ones,' said Abdul Samad. 'He said to him "Tomorrow you'll be marrying the best girl in the village".'

'Yes, by God, that's so,' said the Headmaster. 'The best girl in the whole village. What beauty! What manners! What modesty!'

'What money!' said Abdul Samad provocatively. 'I know you had your eye on her because of her father's wealth.'

'I? Have some shame, my dear fellow,' said the Headmaster, furiously warding off the accusation. 'She's no older than my daughters.'

'What have your daughters' ages got to do with it, old chap?' said Sheikh Ali, seeking to placate him. 'A man's a man whatever his age, and a girl of fourteen's ready for marriage to any man, even if he's in his sixties like your honour.'

'Have some shame, dear fellow—I'm in my fifties. I'm certainly younger than both you and Abdul Samad.'

Abdul Samad exploded into his famous guffaw that came from deep inside his chest.

'Well, let's forget about the question of age,' he said. 'What do you think about the story of Zein's marriage?'

'That's a fantastic business,' said the Headmaster. 'How is it Hajj Ibrahim accepts it? Zein's a dervish of a man who shouldn't be marrying at all.'

'You should, sir, be careful when talking of Zein,' said Abdul Samad with profound conviction. 'He's a man blessed of God and was a friend of that devout man Haneen, God rest his soul.'

'May God rest his soul,' Sheikh Ali added. 'He brought prosperity to our village.'

'And it was all because of Zein,' said Abdul Samad.

'My dear fellow, we weren't talking about miracles. Even so, though—'

'When everything's said and done,' Sheikh Ali interrupted, 'a man's a man and a woman's a woman.'

'And in any case the girl's his cousin,' added Abdul Samad.

The Headmaster kept silent, for he could find no answer to their words; at least from the point of view of formalities the fact that a girl was reserved for marriage to her cousin was an irrefutable argument according to the conventions of village folk; it was an ancient tradition with them, as ancient as the instinct for life itself, the instinct of survival and the preservation of the species. Yet in the depths of his being he felt, as had Amna, that a personal affront had been directed against him.

For an instant he experienced a pleasant sense of relief that neither Sheikh Ali nor Abdul Samad knew he had talked to Hajj Ibrahim about Ni'ma, otherwise he would have been unable to escape from their biting sarcasm. Drinking his fifth cup of Sheikh Ali's coffee, he asked himself why it was he had asked for her hand—a girl as young as his daughters. He did not know exactly. He had seen her one day leaving her house, wearing a white dress, and had met up with her face to face.

Captivated by her beauty, he had given his greeting in a trembling voice and she had answered him with quiet composure. 'You're Ni'ma, Hajj Ibrahim's daughter?' he had said to her.

'Yes,' she said, neither hesitant nor timorous.

Quickly he searched around in his mind for some other question with which to delay her, but found nothing better than 'Your brother Ahmed, how is he?' This was her youngest brother who was one of his pupils.

'Fine,' she said to him, her bold face right in front of his, and went on her way. After that the Headmaster spent many nights with her image in his mind.

Perhaps she awakened in his heart some hidden feeling he had not recalled for twenty years. Finally, unable to contain himself any longer, he had seized the opportunity provided by a slight indisposition that befell her father to call and enquire about his health. By good fortune he found him on his own. After a mundane conversation about the prices of wheat and the state of the school, the Headmaster came right to the point and quickly asked for Ni'ma's hand from her father.

At first Hajj Ibrahim understood nothing, or perhaps pretended not to, and sought elucidation from the Headmaster in one or two sentences which cut into his very soul. 'You want Ni'ma for whom?' he asked first of all.

'For whom?' said the Headmaster with a certain haughtiness. 'For me, of course.'

It was as though Hajj Ibrahim had plunged in a dagger and then pressed down on its hilt the better to make it fast in his heart when he said to him 'For you?' The long and the

short of it was that his visit had been a grave mistake. Hajj
Ibrahim had endeavoured to lighten the blow by making a long
speech about the honour the Headmaster had conferred upon
him by his request, that he would have been the best of son-
in-laws, and so on, but—and this was the important thing—
the difference between his age and the girl's made it impossible
for him to accept. If he had done so he would not have been
easy in his conscience; apart from which her brothers would
have objected. Finally the Headmaster sought to repair the
damage by exacting an oath from Hajj Ibrahim that he would
say nothing of what had passed between them to a living soul
and would regard the matter as though it had never happened.
'Let's dig a hole and bury it there.'

Hajj Ibrahim did not fail him. Nevertheless, the Headmaster, despite the fact that deep down he knew himself to
be at fault, was unable to get rid of the bitter taste in his mouth.
When he heard that she was to be given in marriage to Zein
of all people, he felt the dagger plunging still deeper into his
heart. He was slightly alarmed when he heard Abdul Samad
say to him: 'Your honour shouldn't be in any way annoyed.
If you want to marry, the village is full of women who are
spinsters or divorced, or whose husbands have died—the
most beautiful of women, I swear to you.'

At this the Headmaster really flared up. All his inner re-
sentment was poured out on Abdul Samad. 'Fellow, are you
mad? Don't you know the difference between being serious
and joking? Haven't you got an atom of brain? What concerns
me is the actual problem of the girl—how she can stand
life with a dervish of a fellow who doesn't know black from

white? And there you are talking about spinster women! You really are an oaf of a fellow.'

Abdul Samad guffawed with laughter, pleased at having succeeded in rousing the Headmaster. He sought out such opportunities. Perhaps what had pained the Headmaster had been the mention of widows and divorcees.

'Do you mean to say that his honour the Headmaster, when wanting to marry another wife in addition to the mother of his children, should marry a second-hand woman?' said Sheikh Ali, fanning the flames. 'Really, Hajj Abdul Samad, you are a proper oaf.'

Abdul Samad seized hold of the English word 'second-hand' which Sheikh Ali had employed and proceeded to tease him about it. 'What's that you said, Sheikh Ali? *'Sakan dehan?'*—and he pronounced the words as though they were Arabic. 'Wonders will never cease—Ali Wad Shayeb using foreign talk!'

The Headmaster laughed exaggeratedly, doing his best to try and deflect the attack from his own person to that of Sheikh Ali. But Sheikh Ali, knowing all about Abdul Samad's sorties and the Headmaster's dodges, ignored Abdul Samad's attack and brought the conversation round again to the subject of Zein's marriage.

'The important thing, as we've said, is that getting married is no problem. A man's a man even though he's drooling, while a woman's a woman even if she's as beautiful as Shajar ad-Durr.'

The Headmaster secretly wondered how it was that Sheikh Ali knew the name of Shajar ad-Durr, the former slave girl who ruled Egypt in the thirteenth century. Though ignorant

of it, Abdul Samad found the name pleasant-sounding. However, he was embarrassed to enquire lest he show his ignorance.
Sheikh Ali set about enumerating to both of them the names
of men of no consequence who had nevertheless married women
of outstanding intelligence and beauty. He took possession
of his adversaries' attention for no little time and was filled
with happiness at seeing the astonishment and admiration
that showed upon their faces. He reminded them of the story
of Kuthayyir with whom Azza fell in love despite his being
short and ugly, also the story of the bedouin woman who, asked
why she had married an ugly and uncouth man, said: 'By God,
had you but . . . .' The Headmaster and Abdul Samad almost
fell on to their backs with laughter when they heard what the
bedouin woman had said.

He then referred to the Ibrahimab tribe who were all
descended from the loins of a dervish named Ibrahim Abu
Jibba and how he——but Abdul Samad, exasperated by Sheikh
Ali's being so longwinded, interrupted him somewhat brusquely
with: 'Why go so far as Kuthayyir, Azza, and the Ibrahimab
tribe when you've got Sa'eed the Idiot? Don't you know
the story of his marriage?'

The Headmaster smiled, for he had a special affection for
Sa'eed the Idiot—or was it perhaps because he used to exploit
Sa'eed in getting him to bring kindling and water to his house?
Sa'eed used to sell firewood and to work in people's houses
and would hand over the money he earned to the Headmaster
to save for him. When he had wanted to marry he had gone
to the Headmaster to ask his advice, after which he used to
say proudly that the Headmaster had, despite his lofty position,

acted as a witness to his marriage contract. Everyone in the village knows the story of Sa'eed's marriage and how he lived with his wife for nearly a year without touching her, till the woman, despairing of him, was about to divorce him. When asked about the reason for his dilatoriness, Sa'eed would say: 'There's no reason to rush into the business.' He had, however, in later years, had children, male and female, from her.

Suddenly in the Headmaster's mind's eye there appeared the face of Ni'ma, and once again he felt the dagger stirring in his heart. As though he had not heard all the stories Sheikh Ali and Hajj Abdul Samad had told him, he said: 'But will she marry Zein? That doesn't make sense, my dear fellow. By God, what extraordinary things do happen!'

The Imam of the mosque was also affected by the extra-ordinary happenings witnessed by the village that year. He was, in the opinion of the village, an importunate man, a talker and a grumbler, and in their heart of hearts they used to despise him because they reckoned him to be practically the only one among them who had no definite work to do: no field to cultivate and no business to occupy him, but lived off teaching children for a set fee collected from every family— a fee grudgingly paid. In their minds he was connected with things they sometimes liked to forget: death, the after-life, prayers. In their minds there clung to his person something old and gloomy, like the strands of a spider's web; when his name was mentioned they automatically recalled the death of someone dear to them or were put in mind of the dawn pray-er in the depths of winter, the making of ablutions in cold

water that brought cracks to one's feet, the leaving of a
warm bed for the blast of the frost and the walk to the mosque
in the half-light of dawn.

This was the reaction of those who did in fact go to prayers.
If, however, they were like Mahjoub, Abdul Hafeez, Ahmed
Isma'il, Taher Rawwasi and Hamad Wad Rayyes—those
who made up the band of 'the sinful' who didn't pray—then
each morning they would have that same vague feeling of
apprehension as when casting a surreptitious glance at their
neighbour's wife. If you were to ask Mahjoub about the Imam
of the mosque, he would say to you: 'A hard man with no give
or take to him,' which was a way of saying that he made no
effort to get along with people or become interested in what
they had to say, not being concerned as they were with the
time for sowing wheat and the ways of irrigating it, fertilizing
it, cutting and harvesting it. He wasn't interested in whether
the barley in Abdul Hafeez's field was a good crop or a bad
one, whether the water-melons in Wad Rayyes's field were
large or small, what the market price was for an *ardeb* of beans,
whether the price of onions had fallen, or why the season for
pollinating the date palms had been delayed. He had by nature
an aversion to such matters, and because of his ignorance of
them he was also contemptuous. For his part he was interested
in matters that only a few people in the village concerned themselves with. He used to follow the news on the wireless and in
the newspapers and liked to argue about whether or not there
would be a war, were the Russians stronger than the Americans,
what Nehru had said, and what Tito. The people of the village
were preoccupied with the particulars of life and were not

concerned with its generalities, and so an abyss had grown up between them.

Yet while they did not like him, they recognized their need of him; they recognized for example his scholarship, for he had spent ten years at al-Azhar University. One of them would say, 'The Imam's got nothing to do,' and would then add, 'But in truth, by God, he has an eloquent tongue and is a great talker.' He used to chastise them harshly in his sermons as though avenging himself on them with an outburst of words of exhortation about the Judgement Day and punishment, Heaven and Hell-fire, disobedience to God and turning to Him in repentance—words that passed down their throats like poison. Each would leave the mosque after Friday prayers boggle-eyed, feeling all of a sudden that the flow of life had come to a stop. Each, looking at his field with its date palms, its trees and crops, would experience no feeling of joy within himself. Everything, he would feel, was incidental, transitory, the life he was leading, with its joys and sorrows, merely a bridge to another world, and he would stop for a while to ask himself what preparations he had made for that other world. But the trivialities of life would all too soon take possession of his mind, and quickly—quicker than he expected—the picture of that other, far-off world would vanish and things would take on their normal perspective and he would look at his field and once again experience that old joy that gave him the justification for living. Even so, most of them would go back to listen to him and each time they would experience the same mysterious conflict. They would go back to him because his voice was strong and clear when he preached, sweetly

melodious when he recited the Koran, terrifyingly awesome
when he said prayers over the dead, thoroughly knowledgeable
of all aspects of life as he performed contracts of marriage.
His eyes held a look of scorn and disdain, the impact of which
made itself felt when a man had lost confidence in himself. He
was like the large domed tomb in the middle of the cemetery.

The village was made up of clearly divided camps in relation to the Imam (they never called him by his name, for in
their minds it was as though he were not a person but a
institution). One of the camps, composed mostly of sensible-
minded grown-up men headed by Hajj Ibrahim, Ni'ma's
father, treated the Imam with reserved affection. They used
to attend all the prayers in the mosque and they made at
least a show of understanding what he said. Taking it in
turns, they would invite him to lunch every Friday after
prayers. At the end of Ramadan they would pay him the
appropriate alms and give him the skins of the animals they
had slaughtered at the Greater Bairam feast. If one of their
sons or daughters got married, they would give him a fee in
cash, together with a cloak or piece of cloth. An exception
to this group was a man in his seventies, Ibrahim Wad Taha
by name, who did not pray, fast, or give alms, and who did
not acknowledge the Imam's existence.

The second group was made up largely of young men under
twenty who were openly antagonistic to the Imam. Some of
them were students, others had travelled abroad and returned,
while yet others, feeling the flame of life scorching hot in
their blood, paid no heed to a man whose business it was to
remind people of death. This was the group of adventurers—

among whom were those who drank wine in private and gathered secretly at 'the Oasis' on the edge of the desert; it was the group, too, of the educated who had read about or heard of dialectical materialism, the mutinous, and the lazy who found it difficult to perform their ablutions at dawn in the depths of winter. Strange to say, the leader of this group was Ibrahim Wad Taha, a man in his seventies; but he was a poet.

The third group, the camp carrying the greatest influence, comprised Mahjoub, Abdul Hafeez, Taher Rawwasi, Hamad Wad Rayyis, Ahmed Isma'il and Sa'eed. They were all much of an age, between thirty-five and forty-five, except for Ahmed Isma'il who, though in his twenties, was one of them by virtue of his sense of responsibility and way of thinking. These were the men who wielded real power in the village. Each of them had a field to cultivate, generally larger than those of the rest of the people, and a business in which he was engaged. Each one of them had a wife and children. They were the men you came across in every matter of moment that arose in the village. Every wedding was seen to by them; every funeral was organized and got ready by them; between them they would wash the dead man and take turns when bearing him off to the cemetery. It was they who would dig the grave, bring along the water, lower the dead man into his tomb, and pile the earth on top of him, after which you would find them receiving in the dead person's house those who came to offer their condolences, passing round cups of unsugared coffee. When the Nile was in spate or there was a torrential downpour, it was they who dug channels, set up barricades, and patrolled the village by night carrying lanterns, finding out how people were faring and making estimates of the damage. If someone said that a woman or girl had glanced provocatively at a man, it was they who would reprimand, and sometimes even strike, her—it didn't matter to them whose daughter she was. If they learned that there was some stranger hanging round the village at sundown, it was they who would send him packing; when the Omda came to collect the taxes, it was they who would stand up to him and say that such-and-such taxes were too much for so-and-so, that this amount was reasonable, that unreasonable. If some government representative descended on the village— and they came but seldom—it was they who received him and put him up, killing a sheep or lamb for him, and argued matters out with him in the morning before he met any of the villagers. With schools being set up in the village, also a hospital and an agricultural project, it was they who were the contractors and overseers; they who made up the committees responsible for everything. Though the Imam didn't like them, he knew he was at their mercy, for it was they who paid him his salary at the end of every month, having collected it from the inhabit-ants of the village. Every government officer who turned up at the village, and anyone with any business to put through, soon ran this group of men to earth, for no task could be carried out successfully, no work accomplished, unless he came to an understanding with them. But like everyone possessed of power and influence, they did not reveal their personal inclinations (other than at their private gatherings in front of Sa'eed's shop). The Imam, for instance, they regarded as a necessary evil and they harnessed their tongues as best they

could to avoid criticizing him and would render him 'the re-
quisite courtesies', as Mahjoub would say. Though they did
not pray, at least one of them would attend prayers once a
month, generally at noon or evening, for they were incapable
of getting up in time for the dawn prayer. The object of the
visit was not to listen to the Imam's sermon, but rather to give
him his monthly salary and examine the structure of the mosque
to see if it was in need of repair.

Zein comprised a group all on his own. He used to spend
the greater part of the time with the Mahjoub 'gang'—in fact
he was actually one of the major responsibilities imposed upon
it. They were careful to keep him out of trouble, and if he did
get himself into a fix it was they who would come to his rescue.
They knew more about him than his own mother did, and they
kept a watchful eye on him from afar, for they had a great
affection for him and he for them. Yet on the question of the
Imam he made up a camp all on his own. He treated him with
rudeness and if he met him approaching from afar he would
leave the road clear for him. The Imam was perhaps the only
person Zein hated; his mere presence at a gathering was enough
to spoil Zein's peace of mind and start him cursing and shouting. The Imam would react to Zein's outbursts with dignity,
sometimes saying that people had spoiled Zein by treating him
as someone unusual and that to regard him as a holy person
was a lot of rubbish, that if only he had been brought up pro-
perly he would have grown up as normal as anyone else. Who
knows, though, perhaps he too felt uneasy within himself when
Zein gave him one of his glaring looks, for everyone knew
that Zein was a favourite of Haneen and that Haneen was a

holy man who would not frequent the company of someone unless he had perceived in him a glimmering of spiritual light.

Matters, however, became sadly confused during 'the year
of Haneen', for Seif ad-Din's 'treachery' or his 'repentance'—
according to the camp you belonged to—had weakened one
group and lent strength to another. Seif ad-Din had been the
hero of 'the Oasis', its stalwart leader. When he changed over
to the camp of 'the sensible and the pious', terror struck into
the hearts of his old friends. For one thing, having inherited
money, it was he who generally paid for the drinks, and he was
a useful curtain behind which to hide when making merry, the
village being more concerned about him than them. Some of
them, having seen in him a true symbol of the spirit of unrest-
raint and revolt, suddenly had the ground collapse under their
feet. Seif ad-Din, furthermore, exploited his knowledge of
their inner secrets and so became their most dangerous adver-
sary. The Imam's power was greatly strengthened by Seif ad-
Din. 'The Oasis' had always been his chief concern, regarding
it as he did as a symbol of evil and corruption, seldom deliver-
ing a sermon without mentioning it. Now that Seif ad-Din had
returned to the straight and narrow path, the Imam's sermons
grew increasingly savage and his attacks increasingly strong.
Seif ad-Din was the example he gave every time of how Good
was in the end victorious. The Imam paid no heed to the fact
that Haneen, who represented the mystical side of the spiritual world—a side he did not recognize—was the direct cause
of Seif ad-Din's repentance. The middle camp, Mahjoub's
group, was not greatly affected, for they regarded 'the Oasis'
in exactly the same way as the Imam did—as an inevitable

evil—and were not greatly concerned that some of the young men of the village were drinking, so long as this did not have an affect on the natural course of life. They only interfered if they heard that a young man who had got drunk had attacked some local woman or man. In such a case they resorted to their own special methods which differed from those of the Imam. In their support of the rest of the people in attempting to destroy 'the Oasis', they did not regard their work in the same way as the Imam did; an attempt to make Good victorious over Evil. Rather their view was that the disappearance of 'the Oasis' was a matter of expediency and that they were better off without it.

The fact was that the Imam was overjoyed about Seif ad-Din. He began mentioning him in his sermons, speaking as though addressing him personally, and they could be seen going in and out of the mosque together. Once, seeing Seif ad-Din and the Imam walking together arm in arm, Ahmed Isma'il said to Mahjoub: 'Badawi's son has switched his allegiance from the slave-girls to the Imam.'

The Imam had his own views about Zein's marriage to Ni'ma daughter of Hajj Ibrahim.

Mahjoub entered Sa'eed's shop and placed a coin on the table. Sa'eed picked it up in silence, took down a packet of Players' cigarettes and put it, together with the change, in Mahjoub's hand. Mahjoub lit a cigarette, took two or three pulls, then raised his face to the sky and gazed at it intently, though without emotion, as though it were a piece of sandy land unsuitable for cultivation. 'The Pleiades are out,' he said listlessly: 'time for cultivating the millet.' Sa'eed remained engrossed in taking out packets from boxes and placing them on the shelf. After that Mahjoub moved away and sat down opposite the shop—not on the bench but on the sand, their favourite spot where the light from the lamp touched them with the tip of its tongue. Sometimes, when they were plunged in laughter, the light and shadow danced above their heads as though they were immersed in a sea in which they floated and dipped. After that came Ahmed Isma'il, shuffling along in his usual way; he threw himself down on his back on the sand near Mahjoub without speaking. Then came Abdul Hafeez and Hamad Wad Rayyis; they were laughing and did not greet their friend, and he did not ask them what they were laughing about. That was something else about this little group; each somehow knew, without enquiring, what went on in the mind of the other. Having spat on the ground, Mahjoub said, 'Are you still carrying on about Sa'eed the Idiot?'

Ahmed Isma'il, turning round on to his stomach, said as though addressing the sand: 'The woman must want to divorce him.'

Abdul Hafeez said jovially that Sa'eed the Idiot's wife had come to him in the fields and told him tearfully that she wanted to divorce Sa'eed. On enquiring the reason, she told him that Sa'eed had spoken cruelly to her the previous night; he had told her she was 'a stinking old hag'—just like that—because she didn't use perfume or make-up like other women. When she had answered back he had slapped her on the face and said: 'Off with you and take some lessons from the Headmaster's daughters.'

Meanwhile Taher Rawwasi had arrived and seated himself

quietly in the patch of sand where the light did not reach. He laughed and said, 'The cheeky fellow has perhaps asked the Headmaster to let him marry one of his daughters.'

Abdul Hafeez said that he had set the woman's mind at rest, sending her back home and telling her he would be along to talk to Sa'eed. He had in fact gone to him at midday. When, though, he had come to the door of the house he had found it locked. From within he had heard the gay, happy laughter of Sa'eed and his wife; he had heard Sa'eed saying to her, as though biting her ear: 'Cry, little sister, come along, cry,' at which they had laughed, each in his own manner. Ahmed Isma'il burst into loud laughter, giving out a roar that came from between his chest and his stomach. Mahjoub laughed inside his mouth, making a little clucking noise with his tongue. Abdul Hafeez laughed like a child; Hamad Wad Rayyis did so with the whole of his body, especially his feet, while Taher Rawwasi held his head in both hands when he laughed. Sa'eed, in his shop, gave his harsh laugh which resembled the sound of a saw on wood. 'The wicked fellow!' said Mahjoub. 'How does he manage it in this heat?'

And so their conversation rambled on, a desultory conversation interspersed with periods of silence. Their silences, however, were not so much gaps in the conversation as extensions of it. One of them had only to utter a fragmentary phrase such as 'He's got no brains' for the others to say, 'A man with nothing to do always sits in judgment on others,' to which yet another would add, 'We told you ages ago to remove him from the committee and you said "no",' to which the answer would be, 'Please God, this will be his last year.'

A stranger would not know what they were talking about. It was their manner of talking: they talked as though they were thinking aloud, as though their minds moved in harmony, as though in some way or other they were one large mind. Their conversation would go on monotonously like this, then one of them would by chance say a sentence or mention some incident that would fire the imagination of them all at the same time. Suddenly they would be charged with life, like a bundle of straw that has caught fire. The one reclining on his back would sit up straight, another would clasp his hands round his knees, the one sitting far off would draw nearer, and Sa'eed would emerge from his shop. They would then come closer together, as though towards that point, that something in the centre, to which they all strive. Mahjoub leans forward, Ahmed Isma'il's hands are plunged into the sand, and Wad Rayyis presses his against his neck. It is at times like this that you see them all together, between light and darkness, as though they are drowning in a sea. Sometimes they grow agitated in their conversation and quarrel, the words issuing out of their mouths like pieces of rock, their sentences broken up, all speaking at one and the same time in raised voices. On such occasions a stranger would think them an uncouth bunch. For this reason opinions differ concerning them, according to the moments at which people have seen them. Some of the villagers regard them as taciturn people because they happened upon them in circumstances when their conversation was confined to 'Ah' and 'Oh' and 'Yes' and 'No.' Others would say of them that they laughed with the abandon of children because it happened that they had come across them on an occasion when they were guffawing with laughter. Mousa al-Baseer, however, swears that when he accompanied Mahjoub to the market—a distance of two hours by donkey—he didn't utter a single word. People would keep away when the group was 'in session', for at such times they sensed that its members preferred not to have a stranger in their midst.

Though seeming to behave in a uniform fashion, you would, if closely associated with them for a time, realize the differences that made each one of them a separate individual. Ahmed Isma'il, because of his youth, was the one most disposed to gaiety and did not worry about getting drunk on special occasions; he was also the best dancer at wedding feasts. Abdul Hafeez was the most polite to people who did not think along the same lines as 'the gang'—as they called themselves and were so known. It was he who would inform them that so-and-so's son had married and that so-and-so's father had died, that so-and-so (an inhabitant of a quarter far from their own) had returned from a journey, so that they could go—usually as a group—to offer congratulations or condolences. Occasionally he would attend prayers at the mosque, a fact he would attempt to hide from the others. Taher Rawwasi was the most hot-tempered of them, the quickest to seize hold of his stick or draw his knife in times of trouble. Sa'eed was the best at arguing with government officials and was nicknamed 'the attorney'. Hamad Wad Rayyis had a sensitive ear for scandal, which he would collect from the farthest corners of the village and recount to them at suitable moments during their gatherings; it was he whom they generally deputed to deal with women's problems in the village. Mahjoub was the craftiest

and most astute; like a rock buried under the sands against which one strikes if one digs too deeply, his stolidness showed itself in times of real emergency, when he would take over the captaincy of the ship, he giving the orders and they carrying them out. Once when a new Commissioner came to the district, they met up with him on one or two occasions, talked to him, argued with him; they then came to the conclusion among themselves that he was not suitable. After a month things came to a head with the Commissioner saying to some people that 'Mahjoub's gang' was controlling everything in the village: they were members of the hospital committee and the schools' committees, and the agricultural project committee was entirely made up of them. They heard that the Commissioner had said: 'Aren't there any men in the village apart from that lot?' On discussing the matter among themselves they were disposed to submit to the inevitable, and some of them offered to resign from membership of the various committees. However, 'Everybody is to stay put,' said Mahjoub, and no more than another month went by before the Commissioner was transferred. How was this accomplished? Mahjoub has special methods of his own in extreme situations.

They were laughing, when they heard Zein swearing at the top of his voice: 'The good-for-nothing, the he-donkey.' As he came up to where they were he remained for a while standing above them, his legs wide apart, his hands on his waist. The whole top half of him was in light and they noticed that his eyes were more bloodshot than usual.

'What are you looming over us like that for?' said Taher Rawwasi. 'Either sit down or push off.'

'Zein must be drunk tonight,' said Ahmed Isma'il.

'Sit down and have a smoke,' said Abdul Hafeez.

'They said you were in the Omda's house tonight,' said Hamad Wad Rayyis. 'What were you after? They've married off the girl, so what's the point?'

Zein took the cigarette offered to him by Abdul Hafeez and sat down in silence, blowing into it angrily. 'Not like that, you scallywag,' Taher Rawwasi said to him with a laugh. 'Making yourself out so sophisticated and you don't know how to smoke a cigarette. Draw it in—that's it. Just as though you were sucking at it.'

Zein succeeded in drawing the smoke into his mouth and then puffing out a large cloud. For an instant it remained motionless, then melted away into tiny trails of smoke, some making towards the light, others mingling with the blackness of the night on the dark side.

One of the Koz bedouin approached the shop and Sa'eed went up to him. They heard him saying to Sa'eed: 'Five pounds of sugar and half a pound of tea.'

'Those bedouin,' said Ahmed Isma'il, 'spend all their money on sugar and tea.'

Here Zein shouted at Sa'eed: 'Have the women make some strong tea with milk—freshly brewed.'

'Certainly, boss,' Sa'eed said to him. 'We'll make you some freshly brewed tea with milk.' Then he called out from a window that linked up the shop with the house behind it; 'Make some strong tea with milk at once for the boss.'

Zein was elated and said, 'I'm the manliest chap in this place, aren't I?'

'Of course,' Taher said to him.

'Then why did that he-donkey of a man go off to my uncle and say that Zein wasn't a man for matrimony?'

'The clever lad's getting all posh-sounding,' said Mahjoub. 'Where did you learn all this highfalutin stuff from—"not a man for matrimony," indeed?'

Said Wad Rayyis: 'The Imam's jealous of you—he wants the woman for himself.'

'Is she my cousin or isn't she? He should go off and find himself a cousin of his own,' said Zein.

'The wedding ceremony's next Thursday,' Mahjoub told him firmly. 'After that there'll be no more fooling about and dancing and talking nonsense. Do you hear or don't you?'

Zein was silent.

'Who was it told you?' Taher Rawwasi asked him.

'She herself spoke to me,' said Zein.

Mahjoub had stretched his legs out on the sand and was propping himself up with his arms. When he heard this his body gave a shudder as though he'd been stung and he sat bolt upright. 'She herself spoke to you?'

'She came to me early in the morning at home and said to me in front of my mother: "On Thursday they'll marry me to you. You and I will be man and wife. We'll live together and be together".'

'She's certainly a woman to fill the eye all right,' said Mahjoub with boundless admiration, his voice raised in enthusiasm. 'I'll divorce if there's another girl like that.' Sa'eed came along with the tea and Mahjoub said to him: 'Did you hear that? The girl went off herself and told him.'

'She's a stubborn, headstrong girl,' said Sa'eed. 'I hope it all goes well.'

The rest were silent for a moment, but Mahjoub struck his thigh with the palm of his hand several times and said fervently, glancing to left and right: 'I swear Zein is marrying a girl who'll keep him on the straight and narrow all right.'

Zein as usual drank his tea noisily, gulping it down with a loud sucking sound. Suddenly he put down the cup and gave a laugh. 'Haneen told me in front of you all I'd be marrying the best girl in the village.' Then he let out a great burst of joyful ululation, like the women do at weddings, and shouted at the top of his voice: 'Hear ye, O clansmen, O people of the village, Zein is slain, slain by Ni'ma the daughter of Hajj Ibrahim.' After that he was silent and said not a word.

Soon they heard the voice of Seif ad-Din giving the call to evening prayer (another victory for the Imam) at which there was a very slight stirring among them: Mahjoub coughed, Ahmed Isma'il's toes moved involuntarily, Abdul Hafeez gave a sigh, Taher Rawwasi leaned back a little, and Sa'eed said: 'I bear witness that there is no god but God,' following the muezzin's words in a low voice, Hamad Wad Rayyis blew non-existent sand from his hand.

When the call to prayers had come to an end and they heard the Imam's voice calling out in the mosque courtyard 'To prayers, to prayers,' each one of them got up to go home and bring his dinner. Just as other people prayed as a group in the mosque, so 'the gang' dined as a group, sitting in a circle round the plates of food, with the light from the large lamp hanging in Sa'eed's shop flickering upon them. They ate voraciously,

as men do whose brows pour with sweat from a long day's
toil. They ate fried chicken, and Jew's mallow with broth, and
okra prepared in a casserole, and every night one of them would
slaughter either a small sheep or a lamb. Their children would
come along to them with yet more food, each plate arriving full
and all too soon being returned empty. This time of night was
the zenith of their day, and it was for just this that their wives
worked from sunrise to sunset. The broth would come to them
in deep bowls, and the fried chicken in wide oval ones; they
would eat rice and thick hunks of bread, and thin unleavened
bread made on smooth iron griddles; they would eat fish and
meat and vegetables and onions and radishes. They weren't
fussy about what they ate. At such times their muscles would
become tense, their conversation sharp and clipped; they would
talk with their mouths full, eating noisily, and you would hear
their teeth grind together as they munched their food; when
they drank, the water gurgled in their throats. They belched
noisily and smacked their lips. When their plates were returned
empty, tea would be brought and they would fill up their glasses
and each would light a cigarette, stretch out his legs and relax.
By then the people would have finished the evening prayer.
They would talk quietly and contentedly, enjoying that warm,
tranquil feeling which is also experienced by the worshippers
as they stand in a row behind the Imam shoulder to shoulder,
looking at some faraway point at which their prayers will meet.
At such times the vehemence in Mahjoub's eyes lessens as they
idly roam along the faint, fading line where the light from
the lamp ends and the darkness begins—(where does the lamp-
light end? how does the darkness begin?). His silence takes on

great depth at such moments, and if one of his friends asks him something he neither hears nor makes answer. This is the time when Wad Rayyis suddenly breaks out into a single phrase, like a stone falling into a pond: 'God is living.' Ahmed Isma'il inclines his head a little in the direction of the river as though listening to some voice that comes to him from there. At this hour, too, Abdul Hafeez cracks his fingers in silence and Taher Rawwasi gives a sigh from deep within him and says: 'Time comes and Time goes.'

'Ayyouy.–Ayyouy.–Ayyouy.–Ayyouya.'

The first to utter ululating cries was Zein's mother.

She was joyful for a number of reasons, among them the instinctive joy of a mother at her son marrying. It is a decisive step and every mother says to her son 'I would like to rejoice at your marriage before I die.' Zein's mother sensed that her life was sinking towards its setting. In addition Zein was her only son, in fact her only child; also, his not being like other people, she was afraid she might die without his having found anyone to look after him. This marriage therefore put her mind at rest. It was also an opportunity for her to recoup herself for the presents she had given to other villagers on the marriages of their sons and daughters. People would sometimes be amazed to see her hurrying off to pay her quarter or half pound at wedding feasts. To what purpose? 'Does she think she'll get it back at Zein's wedding?' Zein's wedding was an occasion that silenced the tongues of the malicious—and Zein was marrying no woman from the common people, but Ni'ma daughter of Hajj Ibrahim, which was synonymous with noble birth, virtue and social standing. She would be entering that large red brick house (for not all the houses of the village are of red brick); she would enter with head held high and with confident tread. People would stand up as she entered and would accompany her to the door when she left. If she fell ill people would visit her daily, and she would spend the remaining days of her life luxuriating in care and love. Perhaps Fate would grant her sufficient respite that she might live to carry her grandson or grand-daughter in her arms. As Zein's mother ululated, these thoughts passed through her mind, at which she ululated still louder.

Her neighbours and friends, her family and kinsfolk, all gave vent to their joy with her.

But how had the miracle happened? Accounts differed. Haleema, the seller of milk, said to Amna, as though to annoy her with yet more news of Zein's wedding, that Ni'ma had seen Haneen in her dreams and that he had said to her: 'Marry Zein. The girl who marries Zein won't regret it.' On waking up next morning she had told her father and mother, and they had all came to an unanimous decision about it. Amna shook her head and said: 'Mere talk.'

Tureifi declared to his companions at school that Ni'ma, finding Zein in a gathering of women with whom he was flirting and joking, had glared severely at them and said: 'To-morrow all of you will eat and drink at his wedding.' And then and there she had gone off and spoken to her father and mother, who had both given their consent.

Abdul Samad related to the people in the market-place that it was Zein who had asked marriage of Ni'ma, and that, meeting her on the road, he had said to her, 'Cousin? Will you marry me?' to which she had said 'Yes,' and that it was he who went to his uncle and spoke to him of the matter and that the man had agreed.

It is, however, more likely that things happened otherwise and that Ni'ma, headstrong and independent-minded as she was, and perhaps prompted by pity for Zein, or intrigued by the idea of making a sacrifice—something very much in her character—had made up her mind to marry Zein. It is likely that a fierce battle had raged in Hajj Ibrahim's house between the father and the mother on one side and the daughter on the other. As her brothers were away, they were written to; the two elder brothers, it is said, refused absolutely to give their consent, though the youngest agreed, saying in his letter to his father: 'Ni'ma was always headstrong and now that she has chosen a husband for herself, let her have her way.' The long and short of it was that Hajj Ibrahim suddenly announced the news. It was as though people had been expecting it after the Haneen incident; strangely enough no one laughed or scoffed, they merely shook their heads in increased bewilderment as they looked at Zein, and even as they looked he grew in stature in their eyes. And thus it was that the voice of Zein's mother burst out into ululations and the voices of her neighbours and friends, her family and kinsfolk, and all those who wished her well, joined in with her. 'Ayyouy. Ayyouy. Ayyouy. Ayyouy. Ayyouy.'

Had the wedding not been his own, Zein would have been

at leisure to single out the voice of each of the women as she ululated. This was Abdulla's daughter, her voice melodious and powerful from the many times she had ululated at other people's weddings; though she herself had remained a spinster, yet she always rejoiced at the wedding feasts of everyone else. 'Ajouj ajouj ajouj ajouja.' This was Salama who was beautiful and pronounced her 'y's' thus. A woman of great sensitivity, her beauty had brought her no happiness, for she had married and divorced, and married and divorced, settling down with no man and bearing no children. She was amusing and full of fun and had shared many a laugh with Zein. She ululated because she loved life.

'Ayyouy. Ayyouy. Ayyouy. Ayyouy.' This was Amna who ululated from extreme annoyance—(Do you remember Amna and how she had wanted the girl for her son and how they'd told her the girl was too young for marriage?)

'Awoo—awoo—awoowa.' This was dumb Ashmana; her speechless heart was riotous with joy at Zein's wedding.

Then a blaze of ululations broke out in Hajj Ibrahim's house. Around two hundred voices burst forth together, shaking the windows. Zein's mother ululated and the women answered her; hearing their ululations, she renewed her own. Not a woman there was who did not ululate at Zein's wedding.

The whole quarter heaved in its every nook and cranny and the houses filled up with visitors. There was not a house in which a party of people was not being put up. Hajj Ibrahim's house, despite its size, was full, as were the houses of Mahjoub and Abdul Hafeez and Sa'eed and Ahmed Isma'il and Taher Rawwasi and Hamad Wad Rayyis, also the Head-master's house, and the house of the Omda and that of the Cadi.

'In all my born days I've never seen such a wedding as this,' said Sheikh Ali to Hajj Abdul Samad. And Hajj Abdul Samad said: 'I'll divorce my wife if Zein hasn't got himself married—and a real proper marriage it is too.'

The Imam performed the rites of marriage in the mosque. Hajj Ibrahim acted for his daughter, while Mahjoub acted for Zein. When the contract of marriage was completed, Mahjoub rose and placed the dowry on a tray so that everyone could see it: a hundred pounds in gold, which came from Hajj Ibrahim's ready cash. After that the Imam stood up and let his gaze wander among the men gathered together (Zein's mother was the only woman among them) and said that while everyone knew he was opposed to this marriage, as God had seen fit that it should take place, he asked the Almighty, the Most High, to make of it a happy and blessed union. The people turned to Zein, but his head was bowed. Said Mahjoub to Abdul Hafeez in a low voice: 'What was the point of talking about being opposed to it and all that rubbish?'

All were astonished when they saw the Imam walking towards Zein and placing his hand on his shoulder. Zein turned to him somewhat surprised, at which the Imam took hold of his hand and shook it hard, saying in a voice charged with emotion: 'Congratulations. May the Lord make it a home of good fortune and many children.' Zein glanced round him in simple-minded fashion, but when Ahmed Isma'il gave him a severe look he lowered his head.

The large brass drum let out a rumbling noise as of thunder: they said about it that it could speak. Abdulla's daughter said to Salama: 'The brass drum is saying "Zein's getting married. Zein's getting married",' and Salama's sweet voice broke out into ululations.

The Koz bedouin flocked in to the feast, racing each other on their camels. They were received by Taher Rawwasi, who put them up in one of the houses and ordered them to be given food and drink.

The Talha people came along to the very last man, as the saying goes, and Ahmed Isma'il looked after them and found them quarters. He tied up their riding animals and brought them fodder, then ordered food and drink to be supplied to them.

People came from up river and people came from down river.

People came across the Nile in boats; they came from the fringe villages, on horses and donkeys and in lorries, and they were put up group by group. In every house there was a party of them and they were waited on by members of 'the gang', for this was their day: they had made every preparation for it down to the smallest detail. They touched no food and tasted no drink till the people had eaten and drunk.

A solitary ululation followed by a series; a single murmuring drum followed by many drums with echoing voices. The men waved their hands and shook their sticks and swords, while the Omda fired off five shots from his rifle. Amna said to Saadiya: 'I hope you have enough food for all this lot.' Saadiya said nothing.

Camels and oxen were slaughtered. Herds of sheep were

placed on their sides and their throats slit. Everyone who came ate and drank till he had had his fill.

Zein was like a cock—indeed, as resplendent as a peacock. They had dressed him up in a *kaftan* of white silk which they had encircled with a green sash, and over it all he wore an *aba* of blue velvet, so full and flowing that when it was caught by the wind it looked like a sail. On his head he had a large turban that slanted forwards slightly. In his hands he carried a long crocodile leather whip and on his finger he wore a gold ring in the shape of a snake that sparkled in the light of the sun by day and shone under the glare of the lamps by night, for in its head was set a ruby. He was intoxicated, without having drunk, from the great din and clamour around him. He smiled and laughed, coming and going among the people, swinging his whip, springing into the air, patting this man on the shoulder, pulling that by the hand, spurring someone on to eat more, and swearing to another he would divorce his wife if the other didn't have another drink.

'Now you've become a man,' Mahjoub told him. 'Your swearing to divorce has at long last got some meaning.'

The town's merchants came, as did its government employees, its notables and leading men. There attended too the gipsies who camped out in the forest.

The best singers and the best dancers, drummers and *tunbour* players had all been brought along. Fattouma, the most famous singer to the west of the Nile, sang in her stirring voice:

Speak, O tongue, goblets of praise bring forth.
Charming Zein the town a scene of merriment has made.

They dragged Zein along and pushed him in among the dancers. He swung his whip above the singer and placed a pound note on her forehead. The ululations exploded like gushing springs of water.

Contradictions came together during those days. The girls of 'the Oasis' sang and danced in the hearing and under the very eyes of the Imam. The Sheikhs were reciting the Koran in house, the girls danced and sang in another; the professional chanters rapped their tambourines in one house, the young men drank in another: it was like a whole collection of weddings. Zein's mother joined in with the dancers and likewise took part in the chanting. Stopping for a moment to listen to the Koran, she would then hurry out to where the food was being cooked, urging the women on in their work, running from place to place as she called out, 'Spread the good news! Spread the good news!'

Said Haleema, the seller of milk, so as to annoy Amna: 'What a joyful wedding it is!'

The drums gave out brisk, staccato beats. Fattouma sang:

The luscious dates that early ripen
Steal my sleep and my thoughts quicken.

The men stood in a large circle round a girl dancing in the centre. Her head-dress had fallen down and her chest was thrust forward so that her breasts stuck out. She danced like a waddling goose walking, her arms at her sides, moving in harmony with her head, chest and legs. The men clapped and struck the ground with their feet, making whinnying noises in their throats. The circle around the girl tightened and she tossed

her perfumed and loosely combed hair into the face of one of
the men. Then the circle widened again. The ululations swelled
and surged, the clapping became more vehement, the rapping of
feet on the ground louder, as the song poured forth, smooth and
urgent, from Fattouma's throat:

> *The girl who made Gushabi her home*
> *All night long for her I yearn.*

Ibrahim and Taha, intoxicated by the singing, called out:
'Ah, let's have it again, God bless you.'

Ashmana the Dumb danced, Mousa the Lame clapped,
while the beating of the drums soon slowed down and became
a muffled humming: they were beating out the Jabudi rhythm.
The whinnying noises that came from the men's throats grew
louder and Salama entered the dance circle. She moved about,
circling round and strutting proudly like a filly; she was the
best one at dancing the Jabudi and many were her admirers
as their eyes followed her and she slithered away from them
like a fish in water. The crowd round the dance circle grew
more dense, the clapping increased and the men's voices blared
out when Zein entered the circle. This time he entered of his
own accord; for a long while he swayed above Salama as she
struck at him with her long hair that hung down over her
shoulders, and beckoned to him with her eyes. The Imam, who
was sitting in a group of men in Hajj Ibrahim's *diwan* over-
looking the courtyard of the house, happened to turn round
and his gaze alighted upon Salama as she performed her dance;
he saw her prominent breasts, her large rump shaking and
quivering as she stamped on the floor like two halves of a

water-melon with a valley between them into which her dress slipped. In her dance Salama bent over so far that her body assumed the shape of a circle, her hair touched the ground, her breasts became even more exposed and her buttocks bulged out more than ever. The Imam caught sight of her right leg and part of her plump thigh as the dress was drawn back, and as he turned to the person he was talking to his eyes were as cloudy as turgid water.

'Ayyouyyouyouya' This was Haleema, the seller of milk, ululating in hopes of benefits to be gained from the families of the two spouses.

The drumbeats changed to those of the Arda: two swift beats followed by a single one. The men began prancing about in the manner of horses and the Koz bedouin crowded on to the dance floor, leaping about and shouting and cracking their whips: men of short stature with knotted muscles and bodies that were supple, delicate and earth-coloured, men who lived off camel's milk and the flesh of gazelles. Each of them was dressed in a robe tied round at the waist, the ends slung across the shoulders. As they leapt into the air their bodies glistened in the sunlight. On their feet they wore slippers and bound to the arm of each was a scabbard containing a knife. The voices of the dancers and the beating of the drums, blending with the sound of the tambourines and the religious chanting, all became merged in the adjoining house where another gathering had collected, also in the form of a circle, in which two men revolved, each holding a tambourine. One of them was Kortawi, recognised as the leading local chanter. He was declaiming:

'Blessed be he who takes his provisions and journeys
In the plain of Fereish, seeing the beckoning banner,
To visit Hussein's grandfather.'

People's eyes filled with tears and some broke into sobs, especially those who had performed the pilgrimage and visited Mecca, Medina, and the other places described by the chanter. The man continued chanting with that certain huskiness for which he was famed.

'Blessed be he who takes his provisions and urges on his camels
And who, reaching the plain of Fereish, calls out for joy on
seeing the banner.
He visits Hussein's grandfather.
Before him raisins, figs and water-melons, they spread—
And cups of wine. 'Go ahead and drink', they said.
When he visits Hussein's grandfather.'

The ululations of the women in the circle of chanters mingled with those of the women on the dance floor. Sometimes a group from the dance floor would move across to the chanters' circle. In the former place their feet would be set in motion, their zeal fired; in the latter their eyes would water with tears. So, too, a group would move from the chanters' circle to the dance floor, making a migration from religious rapture to clamour. Suddenly Mahjoub was alerted.

'Where is Zein?'

Like the rest of his 'gang' he had been busily engaged in organising the wedding feast and Zein had disappeared from his sight.

He asked everyone else, but they all said they had not seen

Zein for about two hours. Abdul Hafeez said he remembered last seeing him listening to the chanters.

They began looking for him, though without attracting anyone's attention for fear of upsetting the others. They did not find him with the group congregated with the Imam in the large *diwan*; he was neither in the circle of chanters, nor with any of the dance groups scattered throughout the houses. They entered the kitchens, where the women were busy in front of the ovens and cooking-pots, but Zein was not there. At this they were overcome with alarm, for there was no knowing what Zein might do—he could well forget all about the wedding and just vanish. They split up in their search for him and left no place untouched. Some of them struck into the desert that lay opposite the quarter, while others went in the direction of the fields, right up to the Nile bank. They entered the houses, going through them house by house; they looked under the trunk of every date palm, every tree.

There remained only the mosque, though never in his life had Zein entered it. The time by now was early night: a night of dense darkness. The mosque was quiet and empty. The light from the wedding lamps streamed in through the windows in lozenges of brightness, some of which were reflected on the carpets, some on the ceiling, some on the prayer niche. They stood listening, but heard not a sound except for those that reached them from the wedding party. They called his name and searched in the corners and halls of the mosque, but Zein was nowhere to be found.

They lost hope: he must have taken himself off. But where to, with the whole village congregated together in one place?

Suddenly an idea struck Mahjoub. 'The cemetery!' he shouted. They did not believe it. What would Zein be doing in the cemetery at that time of night? But when Mahjoub went off ahead, they followed him.

They walked in silence behind Mahjoub among the graves, with the sounds of singing and ululation coming to them, loud and distinct, then low and distant. The place was a wasteland except for *salam* acacia and *sayal* trees scattered among the graves. The gaps between their branches were filled with darkness so that they looked like squatting phantoms. The domes erected above the graves of the holy men were like ships on ocean waves. The large tomb in the middle looked mysterious and forbidding. Suddenly Mahjoub stopped and said to them, 'Listen.' At first they heard nothing, but when they listened closely there was a faint sound of sobbing.

Mahjoub moved forward, the others following him, till he came to a stop above a squatting phantom form at Haneen's grave.

'Zein, what brought you here?' said Mahjoub.

Zein made no reply, but his weeping increased till it became a high-pitched wailing.

For a while they stood watching him in bewilderment, then Zein said in a broken voice choked with tears: 'If he hadn't died our revered father Haneen would have attended the wedding.'

Mahjoub placed his hand gently on Zein's shoulder. 'May God have mercy upon him,' he said. 'He was a man blessed of God. But tonight's your wedding night and no man cries on his wedding night. Come, let's go.'

Zein got up and went off with them.

They arrived at the large house where most of the people were assembled and were met by the great din. At first their eyes were blinded by the bright light coming from the tens of lamps. Fattouma was singing, the drums were roaring, and in the centre there danced a girl surrounded by a great circle of tens of men clapping and stamping and making whinnying noises in their throats. Zein slipped through, gave a high leap into the air, and came down in the centre of the circle. The light from the lamps illuminated his face still wet with tears. His hand outstretched above the dancer's head, he shouted out at the top of his voice: 'Make known the good news! Make known the good news!'

The place bubbled with excitement like a boiling cauldron, Zein having transfused into it new energy. The circle of men widened and narrowed, widened and narrowed, the voices growing fainter and then rising again to a pitch, the drum thundering and raging, while Zein stood, tall and thin, in his place at the heart of the circle, like the mast of a ship.

OTHER NEW YORK REVIEW CLASSICS*

For a complete list of titles, visit www.nyrb.com or write to:
Catalog Requests, NYRB, 435 Hudson Street, New York, NY 10014